Ex Libris

BOMBUS
BOOKS

Tell Tails

Edited by Wendy Greenberg

with illustrations by Ann Edwards

An environmentally friendly book printed and bound in England by
www.printondemand-worldwide.com

 Mixed Sources
Product group from well-managed
forests, and other controlled sources
www.fsc.org Cert no. TT-COC-002641
© 1996 Forest Stewardship Council

 PEFC Certified
This product is
from sustainably
managed forests
and controlled
sources
www.pefc.org
PEFC/16-33-415

This book is made entirely of chain-of-custody materials

BOMBUS BOOKS
15 Henleys Lane, Drayton, OX14 4HU
www.bombusbooks.co.uk
www.fast-print.net/store

Tell Tails
Copyright © The Authors 2012

ISBN 978-178035-370-8

First published 2012 by
BOMBUS BOOKS
An imprint of Fast-Print Publishing
Peterborough, England.

Contents

Introduction

Here is an entertaining collection of fiction, faction and fact, loosely connected by an animal theme. Indeed, this connection is so loose that readers may legitimately ask 'is DNA an animal?' or 'do insects count?' We answer in the affirmative because both are here, along with dogs, cats, snails, elephants and many other creatures. Sometimes the connection is so tenuous that it is hard to find but, behind the drama, passion and humour you will find it lurking somewhere.

The authors comprise an eclectic mix of characters and personalities who share a common passion for writing, with the collective name of Oxford Inc. We all met at a creative writing course some years ago, little realising how much a part of each other's lives we would become. It has been a life-changing experience for us all and, as a result, many of us have published independently and all of us have published as a group.

Among the many talents in our group is Ann Edwards, artist, designer and illustrator. She is the cartoonist of the *Chef & Sue* strip which features in the Waitrose newspaper; she has her own range of greeting cards, calendars and gift items and is often commissioned by the Blue Cross and other animal charities to design their own merchandise; she is also the illustrator of this book. More examples of her work can be seen at http://www.annedwardsart.co.uk/.

We miss Isobel Miller, one of our founder members, and wish her well in her new projects.

Wendy Greenberg

May 2012

The Oak Tree

Janet Bolam

Autumn

'*R* *uskin says the only way to see something, to really see it,* *is to draw it,' Liam strokes her hair and kisses her* *eyelashes. 'You should try.'*

At the top of the valley she stopped and made a conscious effort to look around with fresh eyes, with the eyes of Ruskin arriving at Shotover for the first time, easel and charcoals in hand. What would he have seen? The trees were still plump with leaves, although some were floating in the wind. She noticed how bright the colours were, how graceful the curve of a hill, how textured the bracken as it lay across a clearing. Ruskin was right. How could she capture this beauty for herself? She started to take photographs, but somehow this didn't satisfy. She needed more than an image; she needed to scratch below the skin, to feed the hunger for beauty that had sprung within her. Walking slowly across a grassy clearing, she had an idea. She would choose a tree and photograph it from exactly the same spot every month for a year and record how it changed with the seasons. She would do it for Liam. She walked deep into the forest scanning the horizon until her eye was drawn to an oak tree. It wasn't one of the huge, magisterial oaks, but it was clearly very old. Its branches were thick and angular with strong arms intertwined above a twisted, wizened trunk. She looked for a place she could return to consistently to take her photo and noticed three young saplings. Standing between them, she had an unimpeded view of the whole tree and a glimpse of the valley falling behind it. A gentle wind caressed her and a feeling of timelessness settled comfortably around her as she set up her tripod and camera and took the first photograph. She smiled and the tree nodded.

Winter

'Do you always take your pictures from the same place?' Liam's brow is furrowed as he examines her photos.

'Yes, exactly the same spot. Why?'

'Because the branches are moving.'

Wrapping her thick coat around her she leaned into the fierce wind as she scrambled to the oak tree. It was her third visit. The sapling trees that surrounded her were bent almost to the ground, and the branches of the old oak thrashed so violently that her photographs were a blur. The tree stood naked before her, muscular, arrogant. Despite the cold and the wind, she found she was not ready to leave just yet. She ran her fingers over its rough grey bark, exploring the deep crevices that twisted with the grain. As she gazed down the valley through the grey and brown trees, her attention was captured by the movement of an indistinct brown shape. It seemed to flow down a tree trunk and then stop dead. She slowly brought the camera up to her eye and twisted the zoom to maximum. She expected to see a fox, but as she focused she saw what looked like a cat, but it was as big as a fox. It had long pointed ears and tufts of black fur sticking up and as it turned slightly and she saw its short tail. Her heart began to race as it dawned on her that it was a wild cat, could it be a lynx? She pressed the button and took a stream of photos. The cat froze for a second, then disappeared into a sea of windswept bracken. The oak tree roared and bowed to the wind.

Spring

'Stand still!' She is posing for Liam as he sculpts her in earth brown clay. His hand smoothes breasts and runs over the slightly mounded stomach.

'We should be able to feel the baby kick soon,' she smiles.

A carpet of bluebells and wild garlic filled the air with a sweet sharpness. Shafts of sunlight flowed through the newly unfurled leaves of her tree, illuminating the brown earth beneath it. She set her tripod between the saplings, carefully moving the tendrils of new growth aside, so that her view was clear.

The branches of the oak had moved again, opening out as if to embrace her. She scanned the horizon hoping to see the lynx. There had been no sightings since the winter but every now and then, she imagined she saw a mottled brown back rippling through the bracken.

Running her fingers through the fresh soft grass, she rested against the strong trunk of the tree and with a deep breath she inhaled the pulse of the forest. The tiny butterfly tapping of new life stirred within her and, with a smile, she closed her eyes and savoured a fleeting moment of pure happiness. She must have dozed because she awoke to a change in the light and a sharpness in the air. More than that, she had a strong sense of being watched. Looking around, she could see no-one, but the mood was broken so she gathered her tripod and camera and started for home.

Summer

Liam, far from home, sends her poems and songs to sing. She sends him a scan of their baby boy curled up inside her and her latest photograph of the oak tree. She hopes he will come back.

The heat-wave had lasted the whole of June and July, baking the ground, starving the forest of water. Unlike the larger oaks, the leaves on her tree remained green, but she was aware that all around her was tinder dry. Warning notices had appeared all over the woods reminding people not to smoke, to be aware of fire. The oak tree stood alone, seared by the sun, creating gentle shade beneath. Lying on her back, she could feel the baby's head, arms and legs moving, punching,

stretching. He pushed his feet against her diaphragm and ran his heels along the inside of her ribs, he bounced on her bladder. She was safe here, beneath this tree. Just for a moment, before the baby was born, before the strain of being alone became the complication of living for two, just for a moment, she could lay her head down and rest. As she slept, a careless match sparked in the valley below. Fire spread through dry bracken, rolled through the tinder of elder and birch. She woke to a sudden roar as the fire leapt to the branches of the oak tree. She knew she should flee, but she was rooted, unable to move, bound to the oak. Suddenly, from a wall of black smoke, the lynx, ears flattened, body a long thin arrow, darted through the smoke, a cub hanging from its jaw. With her hand moving to her swollen abdomen, she turned and followed.

A Private Passion

Jackie Vickers

They heard the whirr of wings long before the Bewicks flew in to land on the shallow water. The birds rose up at intervals, flapping their wings, then settled down again to preen their feathers and to drink.

'All the way from Siberia.' Paul frowned. Helen said the same thing every year.

Helen did not know what had drawn her to a summer exhibition of paintings of wild birds, for in those days she had little interest in either paintings or birds. A thin, sallow-faced man handed out tickets, his long legs folded awkwardly under the table. She had barely examined the first painting before he stretched and walked towards her.

'Paul Stannard. Robert's friend. I was at your wedding. Shall we have a drink? It's much too hot to be indoors.'

'What about your customers?' Helen asked, as they sat under a gaudy umbrella and ordered drinks.

Paul shrugged. 'The paintings are mostly sold anyway.' Much later, when they stood up to leave, he dropped his card into her shopping basket. 'Come and see me.'

'Why did you lose touch?' Helen frowned at Robert. 'Not even a Christmas card.'

There were rumours, he had explained: a false address, equipment 'borrowed' and not returned, nothing very specific. 'The last I heard, he was living in the back of beyond and passing himself off as an artist. He's only an amateur, they say, which is why he doesn't sell much.'

Later, Helen pulled their wedding album and a batch of photos from a drawer and found Paul on one group photo, standing a little apart, unsmiling. She turned to compare their youthful faces with their most recent family group, framed and hanging in a prominent place. She wondered whether a certain joylessness had not crept across their faces. Helen fingered Paul's card, which she now kept in the back pocket of her jeans. Their talk of painting and birds, books and films had shown her a wider world and its possibilities.

It was the end of October before Helen drove along the remote country road which led to the marshes. Paul lived in a converted farm building overlooking a wetland bird reserve. His studio-sitting room was crammed with canvasses, paints and dirty coffee cups. The window overlooking the marshes took up most of one wall, and its deep sill displayed a treasure-trove of objects: unusual rocks and fossils, postcards, a chipped Spode jug containing expensive but damaged fountain pens. They had spent most of that first afternoon watching the birds arrive, wheeling around before settling on the marshes, where they would spend the winter months. As the light faded Paul grew restless. Later, as she sat by the fire wrapped in Paul's dressing gown, Helen gazed into the flames of a wood fire and thought, 'I must remember every minute, for this will have been my great adventure, my one romantic moment.'

Paul made coffee and lay on the sofa smoking. 'Come for a weekend and I'll cook for you.'

Helen nodded and looked back at the fire where, in the patterns thrown out by the flames, she watched that romantic moment expand to fill the months and the years.

'You must think I lead a very boring and ...'

'Stultifying life?' he suggested. 'I imagine you don't have much choice, am I right? Robert only feels comfortable with the conventional and the suburban.'

Helen did not reply, and Paul, having established his superiority, never mentioned Robert again.

'I must warn you,' Paul told her as they prepared for their first walk on the marshes, 'I can be out here for hours.'

Paul lived some distance away from the visitor centre and car parks of the wetlands reserve, and little lay between his studio and the Wash. The flocks of migrants that alighted on this waterlogged land eventually moved to adjoining fields, now barren, to pick up grains among the stalks and such vegetation as remained after harvesting. It was here that Helen learned to distinguish between Whooper swans and the Bewicks, who, for more than four decades, had brought their families back each winter. That first October, they took binoculars and walked for hours, seeing only the occasional hiker. Paul was both knowledgeable and enthusiastic about the birds: waders, ducks, geese, swans, herons, egrets. He was less comfortable showing her his paintings. His summer exhibition had been a modest success in that he had sold most of the pictures on display, though he had been disappointed by poor press notices.

'Provincial hacks,' he explained. 'Around here it has become a game to see who can write the worst review.'

As the months became years, Helen felt neither guilt nor remorse, largely because Paul's assessment of her marriage led her to believe she was owed something more. They would spend hours together in the autumn and spring, waiting for the arrival and departure of the migrating flocks. Paul had told her that individual Bewick swans could be recognised from the different markings on their beaks. Each year experts recorded the pairs as they arrived with their young. One of the swans hung back from the others, swimming apart. Paul said his mate might be late arriving, as they were blown off course sometimes. But days passed and more and more birds arrived and still the swan skirted the flock, periodically dipping his head into the water and shaking the drops.

Paul now painted less and rarely spoke about art. He had turned to nature writing with surprising success, contributing a weekly column and a series called *A Beginner goes Bird Watching*. Helen watched him as he wrote, admiring the facility he had never displayed with his paintbrush.

'You should have taken up writing years ago,' she told him, while he cooked their meal.

'There are a lot of things I should have done years ago,' he said, gently stirring one of his gourmet sauces.

And Helen waited, hoping he would allude to their wasted years apart.

But all he said was, 'Could you move out of my light?'

In Helen's suburban life with Robert, hinges were oiled, screws tightened, the mower serviced and put away in November. No-one had to hunt for string or sellotape and there were no surprises at the back of the fridge. Paul's studio was everything suburbia was not. Helen never knew whether curtain rods dipped and shelves collapsed because Paul was incompetent, careless or lazy.

'Why me?' Helen asked Paul once.

'That first afternoon, looking at the birds.'

She wanted to ask about the owner of the blue silk scarf she had found at the back of the wardrobe. Did she like birds too? For Helen wanted to be the longest or the most loved; she wanted someone to tell her she was special. She knew what Robert thought. Lydia, who had a complicated love-life at the time, had asked her father how to tell which was the 'right one'. Helen heard him tell his daughter about shared values, a common purpose and a willingness to yield for the sake of the family unit. She had been disappointed not to hear him talk of love, or of the excitement of courtship. Robert's explanation had sounded like a list of requirements necessary to support a structure called marriage. Though her reply might have been much the same.

'Why did you never marry?' Helen asked Paul.

Paul waved his arm towards the marshes. 'Do birds marry?'

'Some mate for life.'

'Most don't.' He smiled.

Robert had given Helen a pair of finely painted china swans for her last birthday.

'They're Bewick Swans,' she said. 'Did you know each one can be identified by the pattern on its beak?'

Robert nodded. 'Bewicks mate for life.'

Helen moved the clock and placed the swans centrally on the shelf above the gas fire, facing each other. Robert watched her, saying nothing.

'I didn't know you liked birds,' said Lydia, back for the weekend.

'She's always disappearing off with her binoculars,' said Tom, from behind the newspaper.

'I've always liked birds,' said Helen, smiling at her swans.

'A private passion,' remarked Robert.

On each visit to the marshes, Helen looked for her lone swan. Paul laughed at her when she confessed to this obsession.

'Where would it find a mate,' she asked him. 'Would it have to wait till it got back to Siberia?'

'He might share one,' Paul smiled.

But Helen kept looking for *her* swan.

'He must be lonely,' she said.

'Or relieved,' Paul remarked and strolled on.

Helen now realised that the idea of a solitary swan had come to mean something different to each of them. As she drove home that evening, a small flock of Bewicks flew across the dying light on their way to roost. She pulled up to rest, suddenly overcome with sadness, and it was totally dark by the time she felt ready to drive home. It took more than an hour, in the inky blackness, to drive off the marshes. Street lights, when they finally appeared, hurt her eyes. She stopped for petrol and saw her reflection in the glare of light from the forecourt, a dishevelled woman, no longer young.

The outside security light failed to work as she turned into her drive and the porch was a gaping dark hole. The blacked-out house stood in a row of brightly lit homes like a missing tooth. Helen had only left the day before, but the house felt damp and uncared for and the radiator was cold. She kicked off her shoes and crossed the sitting room to switch on the small lamp in the far corner. She had not felt any sharp cuts, but the low light illuminated a trail of blood. One of the Bewick swans had been smashed onto the tiled hearth with such force that small shards of china covered the carpet.

The Interview

Wendy Greenberg

I was nervous, like all good candidates. I knew I had the right qualifications and skills, the relevant experience, great references and a supportive family behind me, but would I come up to scratch? I had changed my outfit several times before setting off and now wondered if I looked too casual to be a serious contender. My hands were clammy on the steering wheel as I practised my happy-go-lucky demeanour in the wing mirror.

It had all started with an emotional moment of online selection. Whilst I would happily have chosen any on the page, I looked past Rhubarb, Enya and Cosmo to Toyah (the last of a large litter). However, my choice was irrelevant unless my personal qualities and circumstances were up to par and I could even begin to be considered for 'chosen one' status.

I had completed a full questionnaire about my home and family, holiday arrangements and daily comings and goings. It was years since I had been in this position. I was a pretender, re-entering the dating game, made twitchy by not knowing the rules any more. I had no clue how a decision was made, or by who – would it come down to a 'right' answer to the questions or would it be settled by spurious comments I might make on my attitude to central heating, or brand loyalty? Perhaps a more personal bounty may hold the key – a large lap, un-manicured hands that could tolerate some play fights. Maybe my domestic circumstances would be further reviewed – would my marriage stand up to scrutiny?

There was a continuous background sound that I mistook for a nest of fledglings as I edged up the long tree-lined driveway, still looking for clues on how to approach the interview. The first security door opened, then the second, and I was in, grateful I had spent time perfecting a relaxed look.

'Toyah is over here' was all I heard.

I was on pins and lowered my gaze. Then there was a squeak as she tumbled from a litter of kittens across the room to check me out. Her dark fur hung like a shaggy coat that only a mother could think she would grow into. She was already a big personality – it was bursting from her tiny form. I held her in the palm of my hand and I returned her sage-eyed stare, no longer in any doubt about who was interviewing whom. I hoped she would recognise her soul-mate and that our profiles would complement each other.

I was lucky, of all cats, it turned out I only wanted one…this one…and fortunately the feeling was mutual. A week or so later I drove far more confidently to the centre to collect Pip (Pipsqueak...aka Toyah) who joined our family.

Finders Keepers

Andrew Bax

'This is as far as I'm taking you.' I looked around me and could see no sign of a construction company.

'But where is it?' I asked the taxi driver.

'Ten minutes down there – you'll see the cranes.' He indicated a dirt road, just like the one we were on, teeming with people and crowded with make-shift shacks.

'Why can't you drive me there?'

'They'll steal my car.'

'What'll they do to me?'

'You'll be all right – you look too poor to rob.' As I got out of the car he added with a laugh, 'and too skinny to eat'. Then he drove off.

I was somewhere in a shanty town outside Kingston, Jamaica. Signs of its grinding poverty were all too obvious and it had a reputation for drug-fuelled violence.

But I had an appointment and as I made my way down the road, watched by people of all ages in their many shades of black and brown, I felt pinkly conspicuous. I couldn't understand their thick patois and although most seemed friendly enough, they were clearly surprised to see me. It was a relief when the cranes came into view.

I had come to Jamaica on business and, as was my habit whenever I travelled, I had made contact with a local beekeeper. As well as running his family's construction company, my host for the day also had a large apiary in the Blue Mountains. He greeted me as if we had been old friends and straight away we clambered aboard an old Jeep.

Soon, outside Kingston, we turned onto a single track and into the hills. It was hot and steamy and as the vegetation became thicker and more luxuriant, the signs of habitation became fewer. In the middle of nowhere we came to a tiny police station and, next to it, a shack cheerfully emblazoned 'Lady Godiva's Love Hut'. On we rattled and bumped, and the track got steeper. A couple of hours later we stopped in a clearing, high up on a mountainside; just below us were rows of beehives, clearly very active. Below the hives the valley fell away steeply into misty depths; further away tiers of mountain ridges rose above more mist-filled valleys, receding to the pale horizon in every shade of green, grey, blue and mauve.

But the hives were not what I had come to see. A little further on we came to a little bungalow where an ancient, bespectacled black man ran a thriving business rearing queen bees for sale. In this remote spot, high up in Jamaica's Blue Mountains, he had developed a strain of bee that was exceptionally prolific, industrious and docile, the qualities most sought after by beekeepers. The bees in his breeding programme never flew free. I watched as, bent over a magnifying glass, he held a male bee between his finger and thumb, and induced it to extrude a minute drop of semen; then it died, as in nature. After collecting the semen of twenty bees he injected it into the vagina of a newly hatched virgin queen. It was an operation of incredible delicacy, and it worked nearly every time. From that single insemination, his queens would go on to lay over a million eggs during the next two or three years. On our way back we were entrusted with a special delivery to Kingston post office: 32 newly-fertilised queen bees, each in a cage the size of a match box and packed in a padded bag, mainly for destinations in the United States.

How I came to be on a mountainside in Jamaica followed a frantic call for help from a neighbour a few years before. A few days earlier I had made a polite enquiry about her husband's bees, which she had mistaken as serious interest, but things had gone wrong, and she was now desperate for someone to take them away.

What seems to have happened is this. Pressed for time during a busy day he attempted a minor manipulation with the hives while wearing only a veil and gauntlets. In normal circumstances this would have been fine, but it was a cold and blustery day and the bees turned on him. It was a lesson I never forgot but which I sometimes failed to heed. Bees need to be respected.

Enquiries led me to Wilfred Towler, severely arthritic and devoting his retirement to making violins, far away from his native Yorkshire where he had spent much of his working life as a large-scale honey producer. Next day the weather had greatly improved and in the evening I met Wilfred at the hives, now humming contentedly and at peace. Armed with a smoker and swathed in protective gear, I approached with trepidation but Wilfred confidently hobbled up on his crutches, bare-handed and with only a moth-eaten veil to protect his face. Gently he lifted the roof of the first hive, releasing a warm, sweet smell into the air. 'Ah,' he said, inhaling deeply, 'they've been on the sycamore today!' I became hooked from that moment and, for many years to come, Wilfred was my mentor.

When it was nearly dark we blocked the entrances to each hive and tied them tightly with rope so that their component parts would not move while I lifted them into a van, and then off again in a little orchard at the back of my garden. I was surprised how heavy they were.

Wilfred was delighted to be working with bees again and his enthusiasm and great knowledge was infectious. During the next weeks and months he introduced me to the management of bees in all its complexity and many variations. Above all he showed me that if you are gentle, confident and unhurried, bees will respond with courtesy and forbearance. What other living creature would allow you to take apart the entire structure of its living space –

housing the equivalent of a good-sized town – and do so without complaint? Is it any wonder that they occasionally send out the cavalry?

I learned that successful beekeeping is based on an understanding of the swarming instinct and on replicating nature. You have little chance of exercising control unless you can first find the queen. No easy matter when, at the height of the season, a hive can contain 50,000 workers – all of them her daughters. It is really a matter of observing her laying pattern to eliminate where she is unlikely to be. A grill, too narrow for her to pass but wide enough for workers, divides the hive between the brood chamber containing frames of honeycomb where the queen lays her eggs and the supers, shallower chambers where the honey is collected. The queen begins laying in the centre of the brood chamber in a spiral pattern, moving further to the side as she fills each frame of honeycomb. The eggs look like tiny grains of rice, each attached to the wall of its own hexagonal cell, and within three days they have hatched into grubs. Workers feed them for a further five days and then seal them into their cells with wax. There the metamorphosis takes place and, exactly twenty-one days after they were laid, mature bees cut their way out of their cells. So the secret of finding the queen is to disregard those frames with sealed cells and grubs, and study carefully those with recently-laid eggs. Still not easy with many thousand, often resentful bees and, if the queen is nervous, she will run to the frames you have already disregarded. It took me years to master the skill but eventually I could find the queen almost every time.

Swarming is an essential part of bees' reproductive cycle. In the spring the colony somehow makes a collective decision to raise perhaps a dozen queen cells. This is done by feeding normal grubs with an enriched diet - royal jelly - and preparing much larger cells for their incubation. They mature in just fifteen days and the first queen to emerge will immediately kill her rivals by stinging them through their cells. In the meantime, her mother will have flown the colony, taking with her about half the workers, as a swarm. The primary task of the beekeeper is to recognise the signs of imminent swarming and to prevent it by creating conditions which make the colony believe it has already done so.

So the swarm that is sometimes seen as a dark, football-sized mass hanging from a branch is led by a queen that is almost certainly at least a year old. Collecting swarms is how beekeepers can increase their stock and, providing they are accessible, it is a remarkably simple process. The technique which Wilfred taught me was to knock the swarm into a cardboard box held beneath it and then invert the box on the ground. There would be a lot of buzzing but, within half an hour, the bees would have reformed their swarm inside the box. In the cool of the evening the box, still inverted, is taken to an unoccupied hive, specially prepared with a board sloping up to the entrance. The box is shaken over the board and bees run up it into the hive. It never fails.

Standing proudly on my dressing table is a photograph I took of myself on a stepladder reaching to the top of a hive consisting of a double brood chamber and five supers. That colony had begun as a swarm I collected some weeks earlier but it expanded so rapidly that I had to keep adding more chambers to accommodate it. The swarm itself was huge but mystery surrounds its origin. The queen had a spot of blue paint on its thorax showing that it once belonged to someone who marked his queens to help him find them, but none of the local beekeepers did this. Under the traditional maxim of finders keepers, his loss was my gain: by the end of the season the hive had yielded one hundred and thirty two pounds of honey, three times the average, and the queen survived another two years.

Although I collected many swarms every year, only once did I see one in flight and, to my shame, it issued from one of my own hives; clearly my weekly inspection had not been as it should. I watched in despair, as a cloud of bees disappeared at surprising speed over some trees. But ten minutes later the air was suddenly full of whirling bees again, and they settled on the arm of my wheelbarrow. So I hived them before there were any more mishaps.

Bees are obliging creatures; I became fascinated by their behaviour and the basic instinct which drove it, and the huge numbers involved in trying to understand it. How does the colony make its collective decision to raise queen cells and drones (male bees), and to kill its own queen as sometimes happens? All those bees pouring out of a hive for forage may undertake a round trip of five miles before returning with a load the size of a pin-head; it can take up to fifty thousand bee journeys to fill a one-pound honey jar. How do they navigate their way back, sometimes through wind and rain? As an experiment I moved a hive two feet to one side and immediately returning bees began to circle where it had come from –

they were lost. In another experiment I removed two mature queen cells to see what would happen if I helped them emerge simultaneously. They fought before they had time to stretch their wings; within seconds one was dead and I felt like a murderer.

Wilfred's increasing infirmity made his visits to the hives less frequent but he still enjoyed watching his apprentice at work and reminiscing about those days before the War when he journeyed to his hives with a horse and cart. Something had upset the bees on one such occasion and they went for us as soon as we reached the hives – or rather, they went for Wilfred. The extraordinary thing is that they focused their attack on the black handles of his crutches, gripped tightly by his bare hands for support. I dragged him into some bushes and got rid of most of the bees before getting him home. From an old tobacco tin he took two enormous pills whose effect, if any, probably expired decades earlier. After a cup of tea he declared that he was all right, but I wasn't so sure. Clearly shaken by the experience, he was already suffering from the multiple afflictions of old age and I was worried about how it would affect him. However, the following morning he rang me, as cheerful as usual, but complained that he had been unable to sleep. Not because of the attack, he assured me, but because he had been trying to work out why the handles of his crutches were the target. His conclusion was that they had looked like the snout of a bear, and they had somehow triggered an instinct across the millennia to repel a raid by bees' only predator. Far–fetched? I don't know.

Before long I was doing my bit for Wilfred's violins. One of the hive's by-products is propolis, a glue-like substance which the bees make to block draughts and which Wilfred used in making his own varnish. I also harvested beeswax which gave the violin bodies a lustrous sheen. Although we couldn't find a use for pollen, we occasionally took a sample to analyse under a microscope, to try to identify the plant it had come from. Wilfred was a remarkable character: well into his eighties he took a break from violins to construct a clock from sheet metal.

And then there was honey. Never a priority for me but sometimes I moved my hives to take advantage of particular crops. On one occasion I had them on field beans, a plant much like the domestic broad bean but used as fodder for cattle and which, like all beans, produces a clear, dark-coloured honey. Interestingly, the flower encloses the nectar source in such a way that the honey bee can't reach it; only after a bumble bee has been there first, and cut a hole through the flower to reach the nectar can other insects access it. As this crop came to the end of the flowering period, I planned to move the hives to some late-flowering oil seed rape, a good source of rather sugary honey. I enlisted the help of a neighbour and because these things are done late in the evening when the bees have stopped flying, we went to the pub and maybe we stayed there too long. When we got to the hives it was so dark we could not see what we were doing. My ex-neighbour (he moved away soon afterwards) had disdained my offer of protective gear on my assurance that the hives wouldn't leak, but they did. After dark, angry bees run around in groups, like hoodies looking for trouble. Soon some got under his shirt and he roared; further roars indicated that they had found his tender parts. I had to complete the job on my own.

The trouble with honey is that its extraction is a slow, tedious and messy business. I have a nineteenth century American manual which declares that it is 'women's work', a sentiment which I wholeheartedly endorse. Unfortunately my woman thought otherwise. The nearest she got to bees was when some became angrily entangled in her hair and, later, when I installed a glass-sided observation hive in the spare bedroom, with bees flying through the open window. Until then she had tolerated my pastoral pastime because it kept me off the streets and made a little money, but the strains were beginning to show.

Lifting hives full of honey was giving me back trouble. The end came rather dramatically as I was happily working with the bees. I was suddenly struck by lightning, or so it seemed at the time. In fact I had slipped a disc, putting me out of action for months. Seizing the opportunity, my wife made a cursory check that I still had a pulse and, with steely determination, got busy with the telephone. Brushing aside pleas, protests and promises, she just would not listen to reason. The following day I watched helplessly and in horror as my bees were taken away.

Who Won the first Grand National?

Ann Edwards

Maida Vale Hospital for Nervous Diseases 1865

The old man lay, with blank eyes, unmoving, his breath labouring like a winded horse, in the cold bare room. He couldn't hear the shouts, then screams followed by wild laughter from the adjacent rooms and could no longer smell the slop bucket in the corner, or if he could, it didn't bother him anymore. The label tied to his foot identified him. *Lunatic (pauper)*

The nurse sitting by his side had been on duty for eight hours. She was tired, hungry and sick of ill people.

'This one's drunk himself to death. He stinks. Rotting from the inside out,' she thought as she roughly attempted to wipe away the yellow mucus that kept re-filling the man's mouth with each breath. As she wiped, he tried to suck at the rag, pathetically trying to absorb a few drops of liquid.

But in his head, the crowd roared, 'Come on, you can do it. Come on!'

Liverpool Courier February 12th 1836

A new horse race is to be run at Aintree on Monday February 29th. The race, called The Grand Liverpool, will see ten runners. Two o'clock start. Beer tent and refreshments.

Monday February 29th 1836

It was ten o'clock and the sun was trying to burn off the early morning mist that rose from the Mersey and twisted itself around the two men, chilling their bones. They raised their arms in greeting, approaching each other across the flat windswept field. The movement startled a flock of rooks, rummaging in the short turf. The birds took flight, cawing to each other as they flew across the large field and settled in a wind-stunted hawthorn tree. Their twenty gimlet eyes watched the men and horses suspiciously.

'Captain Beecher, me old cock, glad you could make it,' said Mr.Sidefield, reaching down to clap the smaller man on the back.

The man winced slightly at the pressure. 'Glad to be here. Horse looks marvellous Sir,' he replied.

The Duke, a large chestnut, sported a white blaze down his broad nose, his skin was twitching with excitement as he skittered from foot to foot, his breathing raising clouds in the sharp February morning. He was owned and trained by Mr.Sidefield, publican, of the George Inn, Crosby. If you could race it or bet on it then Sidefield was interested in taking your money. Horses were a bit of a sideline for the George Inn. You got a better class of punter for the horses than you did for racing pigeons, ratting terriers, ferrets and fighting cocks. They generally lived longer too, so were better value for money. The real bonus, for a businessman like Mr Sidefield was that horses had a resale value which a dead ferret didn't. Duke's diet was supplemented by beer slops from the pub and his training ground was the smooth sands of the banks of the Mersey.

Beecher patted the big horse's neck as a means of introduction. The horse rolled his clever eyes at the man as they weighed each other up. Beecher felt his heart soar. Captain Martin Beecher was 38. He had survived Waterloo. An ex-cavalry man'sskills appeared to be of little use to the employment market and it was only the racing world that could provide him the means of earning a wage. Now, after ten years of racing, his bones ached from the falls and he knew he only had a few races left in him. Beecher needed money and perhaps this was the very horse, this was the race and this was the day to do it.

'Me and the lads have put a lot of money on this and you'd better deliver,' said Sidefield. 'Mr. Lynn wants this to be a cracking race and a good show today. Lynn's planning to make more on the booze and pies today than on the race entries. If it works, it may be an annual event. Can't see it myself, people prefer the greyhounds, but he's a canny bastard. If he fell in the Mersey he'd come out smelling of roses.'

A short squat figure picked his way towards them through the mud.

'You talking about me?' said William Lynn. 'What do you think about my grand steeple chase then, Beecher?'

'Looking good sir,'replied Beecher as they surveyed the crowds queuing at the beer tent.

'Coming up to eleven o'clock and look at all the hungry thirsty punters. This is going to be bigger than the Great St.Alban's. We'll show those southerners how to run a race,' Lynn stated puffing out his chest confidently.

'Think you're going to win it then, Beecher? Have to say, my money's on Laurie Todd. Now that's a horse and Powell, that bloke's a winner. With a name like Horatio Nelson Powell he's got to be a winner or a nancy boy. I think you're a bit past it son, Boney gave you too much of a battering. You can ride that's for sure, just think you've had too many Waterloos.' Lynn cackled at his own joke and then having amused himself, decided to push him a bit further.

'And as for your horse, it's worth more as glue, Sidefield. You'd get fifty-seven pots out of him. You could wallpaper that whole pub of yours with that thing and stuff a couple of sofas afterwards.' Cackling, he stomped off in the direction of the pie tent, to count the takings so far.

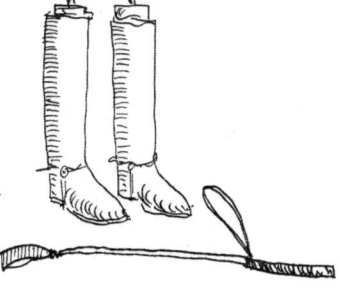

Beecher said nothing but forced the toe of his cavalry boot into the soft Liverpool mud. He'd known Powell since Waterloo. Powell was there when Beecher's horse was blown away from under him. The bits of horse bone embedded in Beecher's thigh, although healed, still ached; Powell joked that perhaps that was why Beecher was such a good rider, being part man part horse. Powell was a pal, a blood brother, a fellow jockey who understood racing, not like the punters, the owners, the trainers. It was men like Powell and Beecher who risked their necks, their lives for the sport. Blokes like Sidefield and Lynn had no idea what it was like, but despite his fancy name, Horatio Nelson Powell did.

It was one o'clock; the race started at two. Powell and Beecher were sitting on bales in the flea-ridden stables that constituted the weighing-in room at this event.

'Have you put the bet on?' asked Powell.

'My dear man, I'm not that stupid, I got some bloke to do it for me. I oiled his wheels with a beer and whisky chaser and he was happy to do it. In fact he said it was an honour, a favour for a war hero,' Beecher snorted.

'What odds?'

'Laurie Todd nine to one. You, sir are the favourite.'

'How much?'

'Fifty guineas. Twenty five each, on the nose'

'Fifty guineas at nine to one, to win, that's over four hundred and fifty pounds.'

They looked at each other in appreciative silence.

Then Beecher said thoughtfully, 'If we pull this off that's our own pub, Powell. No more risking our necks in this caper.'

Powell looked furtively around him checking no one was within ear-shot and said,'So what's the plan?'

Beecher leaned in close to his friend. The hairs from his moustache brushed against Powell's ear as he spoke. 'It's a dangerous looking course, let's not make a move too soon. We'll both keep to the back of the field away from trouble. Let the idiots kill themselves on the first circuit. Keep close to me, but let me lead. Wait until we're on the second circuit. Make your move when we are through the last open gate that leads back on to the race course. I'll start to pull Duke up and slow down. It's far enough away from the stands no one will see us, and then you take the lead. Win by a few lengths, nothing too obvious. Don't worry,you're the favourite,no-one will suspect.'

Beecher pulled away as Sidefield appeared in the doorway. 'What are you two love birds plotting,eh?' The two men looked at him in disgust. 'We are talking through the course,Sir. Neither of us has ridden it. We want to know where the turns and the jumps are. This is a dangerous game andwe need to know what we're doing,' said Powell.

Sidefield backed away, 'All right gentlemen, sorry to disturb you. You just make sure you win though, Beecher, that's my man'.

'Bloody amateur,' spat Beecher, as the rotund back of Sidefield retreated back to the beer tent.

The course, if that was what it could be called, comprised sixteen fences raced over fields, jumping farm hedges, gates, ditches and even running alongside the canal. This was a day's hunting compressed into a few minutes. The course started and finished on the race course proper, which was a strip of sodden field levelled and railed for half a mile before the open country. This was going to be a race that meant risking your neck, with hidden rabbit holes. The riders must run the circuit twice, finishing, by galloping through an open farm gate from the fields back onto the track and to the winning post. There were ten runners, mostly ridden by amateur jockeys. The jockeys were allowed to remount their horses if their horse fell, they were allowed to catch and remount a riderless horse. However you rode it was only the winning that counted. This was more dangerous than bloody Waterloo, thought Beecher.

At one forty-five, Beecher mounted the Duke; the horse caught and ran with the anxiety from the other horses. Dead on two, the starter dropped his flag and they were off. Fields, fences and ditches soared beneath him. The Duke was flying, this was the ride of his life, the horse was unbeatable.

The Duke raced along with the pack, Beecher keeping him safely towards the back, with Powell a length behind him. They jumped over the second-to-last fence and came into a field. The horse pounded beneath him. He sensed Powell getting closer. He could feel the heat from Powell's horse as the ground surged past them. Round this corner, through the gate and they'd have done it. Slow down now Duke. He started to pull back on the reins. The horse fought him for his head, crazy with excitement. The horse didn't want to slow down. Beecher was standing up in his stirrups, sawing at the horse's mouth, making it slow down, when, as they surged around the corner, the gate into the next field and the home run had been closed. Not expecting a jump and Beecher unbalanced, The Duke churned into the mud as he desperately tried to get enough height to leap over the unexpected obstacle. Beecher wasn't ready. His weight was too far back and he caused the horse to stumble and swerve right into the side of Powell. From the corner of his eye he saw Powell's horse jump and try to clear the gate. Then he was over and the Duke regained his head and the horse raced ahead unstoppable, mad with fear and excitement. The horse thundered on with Beecher struggling to control it. The crowd were screaming with excitement. 'Come on, Come on,' and he passed the winning post with the sound of distant hooves in their ears.

Sidefield ran up to him. 'We've won, we've won. I knew you'd do it, we've bloody won!' He hugged Beecher,ignoring the blood and spit from the Duke's mouth that flecked his clothes. 'We've won. I've hidden your two hundred guineas in your saddle bag,' he whispered.

Feeling less than triumphant Beecher screamed: 'What fucking bastard closed that gate,we could all have been killed?'

'We won, didn't we? What does is it matter? We won' said Sidefield, 'the money, it's in your saddle bag,' he hissed.

A shot echoed across the muddy field. Startled, the rooks took flight from the ground and flew away lamenting to each other.

'What was that?' he asked. Sidefield shrugged and looked shifty. 'I'm not sure I think it was Powell's, fell at the gate, must have broken its leg.'

Beecher looked around him. Horses and jockeys milled around him, but he couldn't see Powell. 'Where's Powell'? he asked.

Sidefield shrugged again. 'We won didn't we? WE WON!'

Maida Vale hospital for Nervous diseases 1865

'Come on, you can do it. Come on,' the crowd roared in the old man's head.

'Poor old sod, how did you get into this state I wonder? You needed a good woman to look after you. You'd be better off dead than lying here like this. You wouldn't let an animal suffer like this. You'd shoot it. It won't be long now, old mate, hurry up will you' said the nurse, 'and then I can go home. I wonder who you are and how you ended up here.'

The old man dreamed on.

'Come on, come on, you can do it.' He could see the winning post,he was nearly there. He could hear the horse's breath as its lungs battled to pull more air into them, a few more strides and he'd have done it. It would be over.

The nurse leaned over the grey figure and rummaged in his pockets. She pulled out an ancient battered wallet. She opened it. A newspaper cutting fell out. Faded, torn and crumpled, it was a race report from The Liverpool Courier, dated February 29th 1836. She smoothed the yellowed paper out and read out:

'The Grand Liverpool race ends in tragedy. The runners completed one circuit in safety of this challenging race, but tragedy struck on the second circuit. A gate had been nailed open for the race, but one unknown spectator after the runners had passed through for the first time, prised the nail out and closed and locked the gate. We have to sadly report that Horatio Nelson Powell was killed when his horse Laurie Todd failed to clear the unexpected obstacle. The horse fell onto Mr. Powell killing him instantly. The horse had to be shot. The race was won by Captain Martin Beecher on The Duke, with a time of twenty minutes, ten seconds. The race is set to become a popular fixture in the racing calendar.'

The old man's breath became more laboured. The nurse saw his lips moving but couldn't hear what he was saying. She brought her face closer to him. She felt the faint warmth from his breath on her cheek as he struggled to speak.

'I won it didn't I?'

'Yes you did Captain Beecher, yes you did,' she replied.

Sleeping Dog Lies

Kathleen Daly

There are, they tell us, three great lies in history: the cheque is in the post; I shall love you forever; Human Resources - here to help you. According to this joke, lies are about money, love and business. This story is about a fourth great lie, the one that goes, 'I swear to God, I never touched a drop!' It's about a man called Paddy, his wife Molly, and their dog, who, together lived in a small village not far from the city of Cork, in south-east Ireland.

Paddy had been a steeplechaser of some note and, after retirement, continued to train horses. He also helped with local shoots, and when the game-keeper's Springer Spaniel had pups, he gave one to Paddy. With true originality, the puppy acquired the name Spots.

Spots was not a great gun dog. He preferred to curl up near the range and snooze rather than brave the steady downpours of rural Ireland, though he was happy enough to splash through the local bogs on fine days and leave mud all over Molly's hard-scrubbed kitchen tiles, as long as Paddy was with him. For he followed the man like Mary's little lamb.

Paddy was proud of it at first. 'Will you look at him? He's with me come rain or shine! Isn't he the grand dog?' he'd say.

Paddy trained horses for Mrs Devlin, a local landowner. They fell out regularly, and Mrs Devlin would come knocking on Paddy's door, trying to win him round to come back and work with her horses again. Even Mrs Devlin knew that when that spaniel was around, however hard Molly denied it, Paddy wasn't far away.

Like any self-respecting Irishman, Paddy liked his tipple. There were three 'hotels' or hostelries in the village, though the place only had one street. Paddy's favourite was kept by the 'Boss', a dapper, stout man, marked out by his bowler and malacca cane.

When Paddy was in his sixties, he was diagnosed with a heart condition and the local doctor told him to keep off the drink. Paddy shrugged off the advice but Molly took it to her heart and battle commenced. The village was divided between those who took Paddy's side and those who took Molly's. One half (usually male) was helping him to creep into the Boss's hotel while the other (usually female) kept their beady eyes on him and reported back to Molly. So Paddy had to lie convincingly about his whereabouts. But even if he could take in Molly, what was he to do about that dog?

'Why can't you just lie here and sleep? No one would know where I was then!' Spots just looked up and padded after Paddy.

Now, Paddy tried all sorts of bribery and corruption to keep that dog in the house. First time, he brought Spots a nice big juicy marrow bone, about half a cow's worth. Spots liked food even more than he liked warmth, so Paddy lured him into the shed with the bone and locked the door. Then he slipped off to the Boss's. Well, that dog chewed its way through the door instead of the bone, and hared off after Paddy. When Molly came back from Cork City on the bus, what should she see but this dog sitting outside the door of the Boss's hotel, waiting for Paddy to come out? Molly hauled the dog off home. When Paddy returned, she berated him for breaking the doctor's orders and drinking.

'She must ha' smelt the whiskey on me breath,' Paddy thought.

The second time he locked Spots in the house, that dog whined and barked until Molly came home. The moment she opened the door, he shot past her, and was off down the street. Paddy had gone in the back way to the Boss's, away from prying eyes. But when he came out, what should he see but Spots, pleased as Punch, waiting to greet him?

Paddy was in despair. 'That blessed dog,' he said to the Boss. 'What's the good of me lying, when he's lying out there for all to see, then?'

Next time, the Boss himself took a hand. He went miles out into the country with the dog, but Spots slipped his leash and was back off to the village and you've guessed it, back to the hotel. And so it went on.

Well, the heart condition got Paddy in the end. And that dog was inconsolable. He used to go out every day no matter what Molly did, and would go round each hotel, searching for Paddy. The landlords took pity on him and used to put a bowl of stout down for him. Then the dog would weave his way back to the house, and curl up by the range, dreaming of happier times with Paddy.

On the Origin
Nichola May

Identify yourself.
Show me your phosphate
bonds, that backbone
twist belonging to each
generation. Roll your
tongue if you can,
the phenotype is
waiting
DNA
DNA DNA
replicating.
All it takes is
a   break
a deviation, mistake.
Linked alleles decide, split
blond hairs through blue
eyes. Genes, inheritance:
what's the chance
of fitting in
the
wrong skin;
dark eyes as likely
as an accidental curl
of hair. See that man
back there. It could
have been me.

The Call of the Wild

Jackie Vickers

'He won't get his paws dirty, that one,' his mother complained. 'I've never known a kitten to turn his nose up at fresh mouse.'

'I don't like blood,' Ginger the kitten said. He waved his tail in annoyance.

'Everyone likes blood. Even humans eat rare steak. You're just a fussy eater.'

He thought about the farm animals. 'Pigs get fed,' he said.

'They get eaten.'

'Cows get fed.'

'And they get eaten.'

'Sheep…' he began.

'…Look,' hissed his mother, 'farm animals get fed, they get eaten.' Then she said, in her fiercest tone, 'cats are different, we catch our own dinners. And, remember, no-one eats us.'

He arched his back, stretched his legs and yawned. 'That big fat cat in the farmhouse doesn't catch anything.'

'Lucinda is domesticated,' spat his mother. 'We are wild cats and proud to be wild.'

He wondered what was wrong with being domesticated. Lucinda's life seemed pretty good. It wasn't just the taste of blood that upset him, it was the waste of time. You had to lie in the long grass for ages, just for the sight of a shrew. You had to prowl around in the dark to sniff out mice. Every hour chasing food was an hour wasted.

'I want to be famous when I grow up,' he told his mother.

The old grey cat snarled. 'All you young ones say that, though you won't get to grow up at this rate. Starvation is where you're headed.'

His mother did a lot of snarling. And she was right, if he didn't do something about it, he would starve. But, he decided, doing something would not include catching mice.

He peered through the farmhouse windows. Lucinda was asleep on a chair; she looked enormous and very hairy. He tapped on the glass and howled piteously.

Lucinda opened one eye for a moment, then winked at him and went back to sleep. Reassured, he lay down on the step in the sunshine and waited for the family to come home.

'At last, food with no blood in it,' he told Lucinda, purring with pleasure.

He put on weight and his ginger fur became sleek and thick. He thought his mother would be proud of him. But not only was the old grey cat not pleased to see him, she hissed insults at him.

'You're a disgrace. You've become someone's **pet**.'

Ginger looked at his mother's matted fur. Her ear was ripped and she was expecting another litter.

'You can't be famous unless you take care of your fur. That's why wild cats never get on.'

His mother bared her teeth.

Lucinda was a cat of limited experience, but Ginger brought up the subject of fame anyway.

'You could go in for a cat show,' Lucinda yawned.

'No-one's pinning a rosette on my fur,' growled Ginger and turned his attention to literature. Bedtime stories cheered him, as many were about cats. Most of the illustrations were splendid, though some were only line drawings. He put a paw on one picture to see the effect of ginger fur and wondered whether he could be famous as an artist's model.

Then he heard Dan, the young man who lived in the farmhouse, say, 'I need something eye-catching for a photographic competition, an unusual subject.' Ginger watched as Dan began to spend his time either lying flat in the grass or prowling around in the dark.

'Maybe he could get inspiration from me,' Ginger thought, and took up interesting poses, beside a jug of flowers or gazing up at the stars. He was noticed, but laughed at. Offended, he went to admire himself in Dan's mirror.

'Perhaps I should dress up? A fetching hat or a bow-tie,' he said to his reflection.

Dan came in with a shout. 'Stand there, Ginger. Stay still! Don't move!' and he was made to stand or lie on the mirror all morning, while Dan jumped around clicking his camera. He would tell his mother this was jolly hard work, quite as tiring as mousing.

Then Dan went away.

While Ginger waited for news of his fame, he spent his time practising poses.

'I wish you would settle down,' said Lucinda, opening one eye.

'When Dan wins that competition, I shall be famous and I shall have to look good all the time. I may decide to take up modelling,' he said, testing his claws on the curtains.

At last Dan came in and threw the newspaper down, crying: 'It's a winner, and it's on the front page!' Ginger leapt onto the table and sat on the paper. The caption read: "The Call of the Wild". Confused, he sniffed at the newsprint. Then the picture between his paws swam into focus and he saw a ripped ear, matted fur and finally the familiar snarling features of his old grey mother.

Alan

Wendy Greenberg

He hadn't been home for days when Daphne spotted him sidling up the street, head held high, rump swinging suggestively. She watched as he made his way to the door in no great hurry, not a care in the world. She flung the door open and took a deep whiff of cheap perfume. He had been with that floozy again! Alan smirked and slunk through the door making no greeting whatsoever, heading straight for the kitchen. It was then she saw the new glitzy collar he had round his neck.

'Get your own bloody cat' she screamed down the street...

Queen of the Nile

Ann Edwards

The light from the full moon danced over the waters of the Nile. Sobek watched her. He saw her body shine luminously as the river caressed her. She was a creature made of moonlight, alabaster, phosphorescent, a goddess. To him she was beautiful. Ripples sparkled around her, spray diademed her hair, and lotus stems wound themselves around her limbs clasping her tighter to the Nile's bosom. She gave a low moan as her face turned into the smooth green darkness to meet him and she floated face down.

Harif watched from the top deck as on the opposite bank a pair of yellow reptilian eyes noticed the movement. With an almost silent plop the crocodile slipped into the water.

The cruise ship Hatshepsut moved slowly against the strong Nile current. They were approaching KomOmbo.

Through the palms, the ancient temple (sacred to the crocodile god, Sobek), rose before them. As the light and heat from the day slipped over the mountains, cool west winds swept down to refresh the tourists leaning on the ships railings, as they sipped the first cocktail of the evening. The muezzin's call to prayer echoed from the minarets as the ship sailed gently past the fragrant banks of the Nile. Flocks of elegant white ibis disturbed by the soulful noise leapt from the trees, embroidering themselves onto the reed banks for the night. With a shudder of engines and belch of fumes the Hatshepsut moored alongside the quay as the sun finally slipped over the western bank and night began.

The Hatshepsut was old. Her carcass grimy with diesel fumes, her carpets worn and stained. She was named after Queen Hatshepsut, a beautiful warrior queen, who ruled Egypt three and a half thousand years ago. One night the god Ra came to Queen Hatshepsut in a dream and told her to give him a mountain of gold. Hatshepsut awoke and was horrified. Egypt was rich but not rich enough to build a mountain of gold. If she built the mountain of gold the country would be ruined, her people would starve. But if she didn't, the great god Ra would be angry and turn his face away from them and who knows what terrors would rain down. She decided to trick the god by building him an obelisk as tall as a mountain, shaped at its tip like a pyramid and the tip and only the tip would be crowned with gold. So Ra, looking down from heaven, and seeing only the tip of the glittering obelisk, would think she had built him a mountain of gold. Hatshepsut's obelisk was carved from a single block of red granite, her name and exaltations to

Ra were written up its great height. The tourists would see this wonder on their trip to the temple at Karnak, where three and a half thousand years later it still stands, ninety six feet and three hundred tons of testament to a clever woman.

Despite her illustrious name, the Hatshepsut was not the all-inclusive luxury Nile cruise the western tourists had hoped for. She was a rust bucket. The generator worked erratically and their rooms smelt of primordial damp. The tourists spent happy hours composing in their heads their letters of complaint, demanding refunds as they whinged competitively to each other about the size of their bar bill. To the crew, the Hatshepsut was luxury beyond the dreams of avarice. Food, a bed of your own, running water, electricity most of the time. They felt guilty when they thought of how their families lived compared to this and knew themselves fortunate indeed.

In her cabin down on the water line, next to the ship's engines, Jamila the ship's dancer was preparing herself for the evening performance. She stretched her long sinuous back, arching and twisting, thrusting her hips from side to side. The rhythm of her movements, as she warmed her dancer's body, followed the percussion of the slap of the river against the hull. Satisfied her muscles were ready she tied a scarlet jewelled belt around her waist, fastened an emerald beaded top tightly around her breasts and a heavy gold collar, adorned with turquoise crocodiles, around her throat. As she dressed herself, the tiny silver bangles on her wrists tinkled and clattered. On her ankles she fastened slim chains adorned with bells. Thus embellished, she became not only a dancer but her own musical instrument. Finally, into her belly button she fixed a glittering ruby. Her dressing complete, she looked in the mirror.

Her body was without any pigment. Her pink eyes were fringed with white lashes; her hair was the colour of sun bleached bones, her skin as pale and transparent as moonlight. There was no pigment in her eyes only the pink blood cells reflected from her corneas. There was something almost reptilian about her. She was growing progressively blind. As she peered at her reflection she noticed a worsening. Her eyesight was becoming more clouded, only the edges of her vision remained clear. Jamila was destined for a world of shadows. As she anointed her strange pale hair with rose scented oil and twisted it into ringlets, she thanked her gods for this place of refuge, this unlikely sanctuary.

Jamila was that rarest and most valuable of commodities, an African albino. She had been born to a tribe of women famed for their beauty. Her birth into the village had been a momentous occasion. The midwife had screamed when this mucus covered white maggot had fallen from the birthing stool. Her mother had been shunned by the rest of the village. The tribe knew this to be strong magic and the mother and child was viewed with suspicion and dislike. Across Africa, albinos had become the most favoured prey of unscrupulous witch doctors. Albino body parts could be sold for astronomical amounts to the ill and desperate. If a witch doctor was fortunate enough to catch an albino, alive, the victim would be dismembered, chopped up into their constitute body parts which were ritually buried in the Sahara sands for forty days to dry. Their fingers would be sold as amulets to bring great riches, their tongues to bring good fortune, their breasts would be worn in a pouch hung from the neck to make a child quicken in the womb of the oldest and most desiccated harridan. The man who owned a ZeruZeru body would be rich indeed

She had been twelve years old when the rumours started that a witch doctor was looking for the ZeruZeru girl. Her mother packed her things and they fled from the village at dead of night. They ran for many miles until finally they came to the Nile. They dropped their bags under an ancient palm and lay down to sleep. That morning as Jamila leaned over the waters of the Nile to wash her face, she was grabbed from behind. She struggled and screamed fighting furiously to escape her witch-doctor captor. As her strength was ebbing and his grip grew stronger on her neck, a crocodile noiselessly slid out of the water. Taking careful aim, it locked its jaws around the man's leg. He screamed and writhed, to no avail, as the monster remorselessly pulled him into the water. It turned and taking its prey with it, sank to the depths, a tiny line of bubbles marking its passage.

A caravan of traders let them travel alongside in exchange for milking the camels. At night, around the camp fire, the nomad women taught Jamila their ancient mesmerising dance. A dance that gave her the power to persuade any man she danced for, into believing she was the most beautiful woman in the world. This was Jamila's true magic, not the colour of her skin.

Time passed. Her mother died of a fever and Jamila found herself alone at Aswan. As she walked, dejected, lonely and frightened along the crowded river side, she noticed a sign fixed to the Hatshsephut's gang plank:

Dancer and entertainer wanted, immediate start - apply to Hanif. Jamila thought: 'I would be safe here.'

She smelled him before she saw him. It was a sickly smell; an old smell; the smell of the river bed; the smell of mud and ooze. He was here, Sobek the crocodile god. She bowed her head and her heart beat with pleasure that he had to come to her again. His great crocodile head turned to look at her. She couldn't see him properly but she knew he was there. 'My lord I am honoured by your presence. I am the most fortunate of women that you choose to visit me. Tonight I will dance in your great temple in your honour.' The lights in the cabin flickered and went out.

Hanif, the ship's cook, had been thinking about his wife and children left back at home in Aswan. He worked a twelve day round trip and then one day with his family before the cycle started again. His wife was getting thinner as he was getting fatter. His children had dark rings around their eyes. He wanted them all to continue at school. Leaving at fourteen would be no education. They would not get good jobs. They would end up like him, illiterate, having to work himself into an early grave cooking rich food for spoilt Westerners. Locked in a boiling hot kitchen for twelve hours a day, the food he cooked was often left uneaten on the plates by unappreciative guests. The food he'd worked so hard to prepare, he then scraped into the Nile, while his own family went hungry.

A vision of Jamila the dancer came to him, taking the shortcut as she often did through the kitchens to her cabin. The scent of roses that clung to her hair. There was something repellent yet seductive about this exotic creature. Her pale white body and pink eyes that saw you and yet couldn't see. He wondered if she was his answer. Was she the food for his children's bellies? Was she the roses in his wife's cheeks? He only had one wife so he was free to take another. With a woman like that a man could be rich. He carefully picked out the choicest morsels from the leftovers and arranged them on a plate. This would be his first offering to her.

The generator gave an asthmatic shudder and the lights came back on. Jamila sensed, rather than saw, the movement by the door in her cabin. Sobek flicked his tail and vanished. The door clicked open and the smell of warm honeyed baklava and pistachios filled the room.

'I have brought you these, Jamila, you are looking too thin. A dancer should make the room sway. Eat, eat,' said Hanif, smiling at her.

'You startled me Hanif,' said Jamila, 'Thank you my friend, this is very kind'. The treats melted deliciously on her tongue.

'What will you perform tonight?' he asked.

'Tonight I perform in the temple. The Westerners like this show the best. Atmospheric they say.' From the corner of her eye she saw Sobek smiling his crocodile smile at her. 'This is my favourite performance too, I feel the old gods so close to me here.' She turned to see Sobek better but he had gone.

'They are lucky to see such a wonderful dancer as you,' said Hanif.

The full moon shone over the temple of Sobek. The massive pillars carved with mysterious hieroglyphs telling the story of Sobek. Bored young military conscripts lounged around the ruins. Their unloaded Kalashnikovs strung over their shoulders. Some smoked, some chatted. The group of tourists were herded off the boat and into the temple ready for the entertainment. They gasped at the magical beauty of the ancient building with mysterious shadows thrown against the walls. They marvelled at Cleopatra's store room, shuddered at the mummified crocodiles and glanced warily at the armed guards provided for their own protection.

They took their seats in the nave facing the holy of holies. The lights dimmed and for a moment only the infinite stars lit the scene. From the doorway to the left Jamila appeared like an ancient apparition, her pale body hidden by a black Malaya. Her arms were above her in the Egyptian temple posture. No one stirred. It was as if time had rewound and they were in ancient Egypt, witnesses to a profound mystery. As the tabla and rababa started to play their winding pounding pulsing rhythms, Jamila's body undulated in ecstasy. The audience was now completely transformed, washed clean from the shallow, greedy creatures of the day, to worshippers of this primeval force of the night. They were bathed and transformed in the moonlight.

Hanif watched from the shadows. Yes she was the answer, she would be his. She would not come willingly, but she would get used to the idea eventually. His wife would help calm her. He had bought some strong sleeping pills from Abdul the purser. The tourists were always leaving medicines lying around in their cabins. He could keep her drugged and hidden in the ceiling space above his cabin till they got back to Aswan. Then it would be easy to smuggle her off the boat. His wife would know what to do with her. He salivated at the prospect.

The last note of the tabla hung in the air and Jamila stood motionless, then shockingly she fell to the floor, hidden again by her malaya. It was as if she had vanished. The audience leapt to their feet in rapturous applause and there was silence.

The tourists drifted back to the boat enjoying the breeze as they walked along the banks of the Nile. Behind them the temple of KomOmbo settled back into the darkness and pulled its mysteries closer to it.

Back in her cabin Jamila sponged the sweat from her body and then fell exhausted onto her bunk. She found the performances more and more draining. She could hear the ship starting to settle for the night. The tourists called their goodnights to each other, doors slammed. She could faintly smell tomorrow's bread baking in the ovens. The air conditioning hummed. The ship rocked comfortingly from side to side, and she fell asleep cradled in the boat's arms.

Up in the kitchens, Hanif was pummelling the last of the sweet dough ready for the morning. His massive forearms beat and stretched the mixture until it was silky smooth. He carefully shaped it into delicate crescents and placed it into the ovens. As he worked he hummed the ancient desert tunes Jamila had danced to. He must wait, he thought, he must be patient, he would know when the time was right, the time he could make her his. As he had finished putting the last tray into the ovens, the generator gave its habitual grunt and stopped. The ship was plunged into darkness. Hanif cursed, his bread would be ruined and he would have to start again.

Down in her cabin Jamila stirred and awoke. The room was suffocatingly hot. The air conditioning had stopped. She tossed and turned but could not get comfortable. Her poor weak eyes got accustomed to the dark. She lay there for a few minutes willing the generator to come on again and the cool air to start. It didn't. With a sigh she got up, pulled on a thin cotton robe and went out of the cabin.

Hanif too waited for the generator to start again. The hammering and voices coming from the engine room meant that this was a bigger problem than normal. Experience told him it could take at least half an hour before the boys had fixed it. He might as well go and have a smoke.

Up on the deck Jamila leaned her forehead against the railing to cool it. The night air was like a kiss against her hot skin. A skein of Nile geese called to each other as they flew overhead. Hanif saw her. She didn't hear him but she felt the whistle of the air as the punch came towards her. She turned to look at him in surprise. His fist still scented with sweet dough hit her on the side of the head. Rage surged through Hanif's body, rage at his lousy life, he realised he'd enjoyed hitting her. He hit her again. She fell. She tried to pull herself up. He hit her in the stomach and the force of it lifted her up and she lay draped along the railings, her wrap opening to show her pale body. He hit her in the face. Her head lolled backwards, her fingers grasped the railings and she tried to pull herself away from him. He grabbed her but she slipped from him. All he was left holding was her wrap as she fell, naked, backwards into the water.

The cool water felt wonderful to Jamila. She wasn't frightened. She knew he was there. There was no need to struggle he would come for her. The light from the full moon danced over the waters of the Nile. Lord Sobek the crocodile god heard her. He saw her body shine luminously as the river stroked her. She was a creature made of moonlight, alabaster, phosphorescent, a goddess. To him she was beautiful. Ripples sparkled around her, spray diademed her hair. Lotus stems wound themselves around her limbs clasping her tighter to the Nile's bosom. She gave a low moan as her face turned into the smooth green darkness to meet him and she floated face down.

Harif watched from the top deck, as on the opposite bank a pair of yellow reptilian eyes noticed the movement. With an almost silent plop the crocodile slipped into the water.

Midsummer

Kathleen Daly

The sorrel pony shifted his weight, vibrating the tentacles of tubes and the drips swinging from the roof. There was a pale froth round his mouth. The stall smelled of antiseptic and fear. His eyes flickered white, then the pupils engulfed them again. The day dripped away, hour after turgid hour. A blackbird's song liquefied in the stillness.

Sol couldn't stand it any longer. He strode across the lawn, to the main clinic.

'He's too far gone,' he said to his colleague Andrea.

'He's strong. Pity he isn't younger, but he's fit,' the older woman insisted. 'Besides, his owner's devoted to him. Up with him all night.'

'She's not there now.'

'Gone off for some breakfast, I expect. Maggie suggested it. We don't know how much longer this will go on.'

Maggie was a good veterinary nurse, but in Sol's view, she would have done better to keep her advice to herself.

'Why not just get it over with now?' he snapped. Her eyes widened and her lips contracted.

'Do you think I'd have operated if I didn't think he had a fighting chance?'

Sol knew he'd gone too far. He'd only recently joined the practice and didn't want to alienate his senior colleague. He peeled off his latex gloves and strode away, mentally cursing Andrea's optimism, and owners who thought they were doing the best for their animals but were really prolonging their suffering.

When he looked in later that afternoon, the sorrel pony was no better, though the owner was back. He shouldn't interfere, the patient was Andrea's, but he couldn't help himself.

'It's not fair to leave him in that much pain and in this heat,' he said to the slight woman leaning over the stall. She was a bit older than Andrea, he guessed. She wasn't bad-looking for her age. Her hair was prematurely white but it suited her pale complexion. Fine lines around her eyes, nose a little sharp, slightly reddened. Her eyes were green. A school-teacher maybe, or in local government. She looked sensible, as if she would listen to reason.

'It's true,' he said, 'he's going downhill fast.'

'Andrea suggests another operation.'

'Folly!' he thought, but said as gently as he could, 'He's not up to it in my opinion. Look at him.'

The animal was flecked with sweat, trying to box-walk but tugged back by the tubes, like a horse on a carousel. The curse of modern veterinary medicine personified. In the old days, if an equid didn't pull round from colic in a few hours, that was it. No fancy operations. The next box was empty. Another of Andrea's cases, a thoroughbred they'd put down earlier. Owner gave the go-ahead from abroad. Better that way, less interference and emotion. A clear, rational decision that's in the animal's best interests.

'Can you do anything for the pain?'

'The painkiller's probably wearing off. I'll check when he's due another one.'

He was glad of the excuse. Why did they put themselves and the animals through it?

Maggie looked up from the sink.

'Little sorrel no better? Such a shame, a real trooper. Doing so well the first two days after the op. We even took him out for a pick of grass yesterday. You just can't tell, can you?' As she pushed her blonde fringe out of her eyes, drops from her hands trickled over her cheeks.

'Where's Andrea?' he said.

'With that Arab mare at the Rowley stud, that's having trouble dropping a foal. She should be back by now.' She checked her watch. 'Better give the sorrel another shot.'

'We should end it.'

She frowned. 'Have you checked with Andrea? Thought not. Honestly, Sol. Here, take my mobile. The number's in there.'

He stabbed the buttons. The voicemail message began its drone. He left a curt response and switched off. Maggie's slightly protruding pale blue eyes quizzed him.

'I'll give the analgesic,' he grunted.

She nodded. 'That will buy him an hour or so of peace.'

The woman was in the stall, coaxing the restless pony. It swung towards her voice, then resumed its circling. Sol clipped on a lead rope and asked her to hold it and soothe the animal, as he slipped the needle into the vein.

'We'll need to change the drip soon too.' He glanced down at the serum seeping from the stitches in the pony's belly and soaking the shredded paper shavings pale pink.

The woman said something Sol couldn't catch. As he twitched round, she spoke again.

'It's over. I can't stand this.'

He gazed at her, uncomprehending. Then relief made him rattle, 'it will be very quick. Instant really. He won't suffer. If you want to leave … '

'No, I have to be here. See him out. That's all I can do for him now, isn't it?'

Sol nodded. He wanted to reassure her that she'd made the right decision, but in the dry atmosphere and heat, he couldn't get the words out.

'I want him,' she said, 'to have five minutes of normality. Without the tubes. Outside.'

Sol reached up and started to remove the drip bags and tubing.

'Can he have a drink now?' she said.

Sol nodded. While the drip was in, the pony wasn't allowed a water bucket. In the silence, they could hear the breath slowing, see flanks rising and falling in a steady rhythm. The pony's head drooped.

'Give him a few more minutes. So the painkiller can work.'

'I had him as a yearling,' she said. 'He's eighteen now.'

'That's a long time.' She would have been in her twenties then. Half a lifetime away.

'The year my father died,' she said. Sol cringed. He didn't want to know. The midsummer heat pulsed through the stables. It was nearly six in the evening but it must be pushing eighty outside. She stroked the pony's wet neck. Sweat trickled down his own back.

'I was on holiday. It was all over when I got back. A brain tumour diagnosed after I went away. I'd thought he just had flu. I still see him there, in that bed, shrunken.'

Sol nodded. What could he say?

'I'd like to think Casper remembered the grass.' She rubbed the pony's white blaze.

'I'll leave you for a while. He can graze on the green strip near the paddocks. There's a trough out there for him, too.'

Beyond the surgery window, the world simmered. The pony lowered his head, clipped half-heartedly at the grass, followed his owner to the water, nosed it, left it. Woman and animal stood, tranquil, her arm over his neck, he nuzzling her other hand. It could be one of those sentimental pictures for a jigsaw, thought Sol, wrenching a syringe from the cupboard. Beyond the white rails, a stilt-legged foal tottered after its mother.

❧❀☙

'There's just one more,' said Maggie, looking up from the phone. 'A routine vetting. Out at Barrows Farm. Can you do that, Sol?'

Sol nodded. 'Tell them I'll be there at 10.'

'And it's Lindy's birthday party, remember. Don't be late.'

'Unless there's another emergency.'

'Andrea said she'd cover it.'

'Unless there are two emergencies, then.'

Maggie lobbed a ball of paper at him. As if he'd miss their daughter's party. Pity it was such a grizzly day. No chance of getting the kids outside, then. All those toddlers loose in the house didn't bear thinking about. No wonder Maggie wanted him there.

Barrows was on the edge of the Ridgeway, a relaxed livery yard of about twenty horses, run by the Meads, an elderly lady and her son.

'That's the one,' Marigold Mead said, pointing to a little chestnut. 'He's mine. Got him as a youngster from the pony sales. It was me or the meat market. What a job we had even to get him in the horsebox, poor little chap. He's come on nicely. The woman who's buying him's had him on loan, so she knows the ins and outs of it. Bit green still. No malice in him, mind, just mischief.'

The prospective owner was feeding carrots to the pony. She smiled as she turned to look at Sol.

'I'm glad it's you,' she said. 'Do you recognise me?'

Sol nodded. She looked vaguely familiar, but he really hadn't any idea. Maggie was much better with people. He only remembered the animals.

'You were so kind to me. About three years ago. When I lost my other pony. A little sorrel. It was about this time of year, in fact. It took me ages to get over it. But here I am, back again. I don't know why we do it really, do you?'

She pushed her white hair back and put on her riding hat. Sol ran his hand down the pony's legs, to avoid meeting her eye.

Animal Crackers

Veronica Mackinnon

Snail

I know a snail who's very bright,
He's got a PhD.
He went to university
And studied botany.

His brains exceed his beauty:
His eyes stick up on pegs.
He slides along upon his tum,
He hasn't any legs.

But he's a snail of many parts,
A mollusc most astute.
He lectures at the RHS
On vegetables and fruit.

Pug

I was born to be superior,
I'm an Emperor, an Earl.
It's because my nose is pretty
And my tail's a perfect curl.

I'm far better than the others;
I don't hunt or round up sheep.
How vulgar to be working
When one could be sound asleep!

My bloodline is unblemished,
For we were the dogs of kings.
I stride out with the arrogance
Of one who knows these things.

My ears are blackest velvet
And my coat a dense, fur rug.
I am the greatest canine,
An indomitable pug!

Jack Russell

I wanted one with nice short hair;
Instead it sprouted everywhere.

I hoped his tail would stick out straight,
But up it curled – a vulgar trait.

I tried to teach him 'Sit' and 'Stay'.
He turned his back and walked away.

I told him that he must NOT bite,
But 'Posty' got an awful fright!

We all prayed that he wouldn't yap;
He barks all day without a gap.

I wanted him to scare the rats,
Not persecute the local cats

I want a dog that's clean and neat,
Not one with fleas and dirty feet.

And when he's had his monthly bath
He rolls in something, for a laugh.

But when he's happy, what a grin!
Jack Russell monster, we love him.

Cat

He's a tiger in the mornings
When he pounces on my bed
He's a serpent when he's hungry
And he snakes around my legs.
He's a fire-breathing dragon
If he spots the dog next door;
He's as playful as a mongoose
Chasing toys across the floor.
He's a lion, a bear, a panther,
A thoroughbred, so sleek,
But he's just my little puss-cat
When he's curled up, fast asleep.

All that Glitters

Janet Bolam

The glitter ball shines distorted square spots of light onto the glitterati assembled at this year's Jupiter Awards. The diamonds and diamante bling right back. The host for the evening is opening an envelope, building the tension, ready to announce the Album of the Year.

'...and the winner is...,' obligatory wait... 'McAvoy with Arc Unfinished !!!!!'

The audience explodes as the cameras swing to McAvoy's table. A stunning dark-haired beauty, Keira Cox, releases him from a kiss, then he picks his way towards the stage to receive his award. He remembers to thank his agent, his Mum and Dad and all the people who had helped him on this 'incredible journey'.

Cut to the minstrels gallery where the commentator and her guests react with pleasure. They agree he is a worthy winner.

'...this extraordinary first album is awarded its place in history.'

'...the timeless themes of Love and Loss treated with such conviction and originality...'

Cut back to the stage as McAvoy, guitar in hand, plays the first chords of 'Maybe We Could Try'. His dark hair is shiny and tousled. He looks straight into the camera with limpid eyes and melts every girl's heart. He starts to sing.

Me, in the Ladies loo at 'The Chequers', leaning into a small mirror reapplying my lipstick. The eyes are tired, the skin sallow and my hands are shaking. I put away my make-up bag and practise smiling. I walk back to my table of friends.

'Hey Joanie! Rick nailed it!' my friend nods her head towards the large screen and there is Rick, or McAvoy as he is now known, singing a song about me. He used to mean it, but that was months ago. A reporter stops Rick and Keira Cox, his current girlfriend, as they make their way back across the red carpet to their waiting car. My friends, with an eye on me, playfully jeer at the image, and I feel my sister's hand as she places it on my back in silent support. I should be used to it by now.

I go home and share chocolate digestives with Fleur. I know it's not good for her, but she looks up with those eyes and wags her tail wildly, hardly able to contain herself. Fleur is my dog, although she used to be ours. Rick's and mine. She was about a year old when we got her from the Blue Cross. Part Border Collie, part Irish Setter, with a possibility of Cocker Spaniel in there somewhere, makes her one pretty special mongrel! I looked at the framed photo I had of the three of us on holiday in Pembrokeshire that I somehow couldn't bear to take down. It was hard to accept that we had once been that happy.

'Well, Fleur,' I tell her as I roll my hands in her long fur 'it can't all be bad. It just feels like it.'

McAvoy wakes with a thumping hangover. Keira is long gone. He reaches for the remote and flicks on Breakfast Today. The post-show interview on the red carpet flashes in front of him like someone else's memory. Keira looks good. He drifts back to sleep. The phone wakes him.

'Rick, it's Marva. Have I had a morning! Have you seen the papers? They're calling you the new Bob Dylan. A curse, a curse. You are the one and only McAvoy! Anyway darling, offers are pouring in! Don't forget, you're doing an interview for *The Culture Show* in two hours and then I've lined up Rolling Stone, Q and NME. The Mail on Sunday wants an exclusive. I told them to put that where the sun don't shine! The other papers will want you too. Everyone wants you sweetheart. And Rick, you're going to love this….*OK!* wants to do a feature on you and Keira. An agent's dream.My two favourite gorgeous, gorgeous clients together. I'll make sure this runs and runs! Speaking of which, I'm late for a meeting …'

'This should be the best morning of my life' he reminds himself as he steps over his clothes and heads for the shower.

I watch breakfast TV even though I don't want to. There he is with Keira. I notice how she seems to lean in to him, how he seems anxious. I know that body language well. I know that walk, that smile he gives when he is uncertain and I know that all the hard work to put my life back together again has been ripped apart, as I listen to song after song about us. I hear them on the radio, the TV, tunes underscoring sitcoms and adverts and it's even been used in that film, *Marching Home,* which is longlisted for an Oscar. I'm angry that he calls the album Arc Unfinished and that he plays stupid games in interviews.

'Why is the album called Arc Unfinished?'

'Because it's unfinished...'

'You mean the relationship you write about is unfinished?'

'In a sense, yes. We go our separate ways... but it doesn't always mean the end of the story, does it?'

It's got Marva and her showbiz, honey glaze all over it and he is fool enough to do as she says.

When we broke up nine months ago, I was bereft. He'd been on tour with Modal Validation for months and it was his birthday, so I planned a surprise visit. I bought a ticket for the concert and my plan was to go backstage after the performance and surprise him. I had booked a discreet table at *Gaston's* and was looking forward to some time together. Sitting in the dark anonymity of the auditorium, I watched him alone on the stage with his guitar and I almost choked with love. Then at the end of his set, Keira joined him for a duet.

The chemistry between them sizzled, and when they gave each other a kiss at the end of the song to the cheers of the audience, I knew it was real. I went home.

Strangely, the rows we had when we were breaking up were not about us, but about who took Fleur. Of course, it made sense for me to keep her because I live in one place and I've been proved right; Rick has been on the road pretty solidly ever since we split.

'I want Rick lying in the grass, here, and the dog, here, next to him.' Sam, the music video producer is talking to her assistants, who are positioning them for the last of the filming. Fleur lays her head on Rick's chest, just like she used to do. 'Hey! That's great. Let's keep that and we'll pan round, move in and then Rick, get the dog to wink.'

'I can't make the dog wink.'

'But you told me the dog winks!'

'I know!'

'Then what's the problem?'

'Only Joanie can make her wink'

'OK! Someone find Joanie! Let's get her here right now! We're losing light!'

I've been keeping myself to myself watching the filming from the sidelines. So far, Rick and I have exchanged pleasantries, nothing more. He wanted to use Fleur in this video and it would have been unfair not to allow it. Rick and I discovered that Fleur would wink if I blew on her nose and clicked my fingers. She would only do it for me, but she did it every time. I remember the day we taught her and how Rick and I could hardly stand up for laughing.

Sam was checking camera angles as I approached. Rick had explained the procedure, so I guess they were working out how to get a doggy wink, with me out of shot. I crouched down to level with Fleur and blew, but all she did was perk up her ears and try to scramble over Rick to lick my face.

'The problem is I'm too far away from her when I blow on her nose, so she doesn't realise it's what she's meant to do!'

Sam, who has sworn never to work with animals or rock stars again, yells 'You can move a foot nearer, then blow as hard as you can!'

I tunnel closer and Rick and I are inches apart. 'Hi you', he whispers.

Fleur beats her tail, and finally, mercifully, looks straight at the rolling camera and gives a huge wink and a couple of happy yaps for good measure.

'Got it! That's a wrap!' shouts Sam and we all relax.

My eyes meet Rick's and for a second, I feel a flame of hope. 'You haven't changed', he smiles.

'You have', I say, as I turn away to hide unwanted tears.

The floor of Rick's living room is covered with a tangled chaos of cables, running from computer to keyboard, to amplifiers and banks of speakers. Plates from meals long forgotten balance on the sofa arm, or squat on the jumbled coffee table. He is alone in the middle of devastation, in a sea of discarded writing. The Jupiter Award mocks him from its lofty mount on the wall, and the now familiar feeling of anxiety ripples through him. What to do? It should be easier than this. He has some songs for his next album, of course he has, but somehow they feel formulaic, without soul. Things used to be clear to him; he sang songs and people liked them. Now he feels like a cog in a Marva driven publicity machine, pushing this guy called McAvoy, that he realises he doesn't know very well.

OK! Magazine lies discarded in the detritus of the kitchen, turned to the three-page article about Keira and him. Pictures of them walking through a field –'Work, rest and play, Keira and McAvoy Have It All!', singing on stage together, 'Rock solid duo', then arm-in-arm leaning against a cliff on a deserted windswept beach, 'We love to have time to make our own music'. Marva had supplied the quotes of course. When Keira saw them she laughed, but the whole thing made Rick feel uncomfortable and he had told Marva so. 'What do you expect?' she remarked, 'No-one recognises themselves in rags like this! Take a leaf out of Keira's book. She knows these things for what they are. It's all good publicity and you'll thank me when you get your next pay cheque!'

Rick flicks through his ipod and finds Peggy Lee. 'Is that all there is?' she sings. 'If that's all there is my friend, then lets keep dancing'. Rick sways to the music and opens another beer.

Fleur has been ill. She started by throwing up all over my bed, and was still not eating a couple of days later. I took her to the vet and she told me to keep an eye on her and if she got worse to bring her back. A day later, she was staggering around unable to walk on her hind legs and was shaking. Trying not to panic, I rushed her back to the vet, who told me she either had a kidney infection or that she'd been poisoned and her kidneys were failing. The vet explained that if Fleur had a bacterial infection, then a course of antibiotics would do the trick, but if she's been poisoned, then there we would just have to watch and wait. I will never forget that moment as long as I live; all I heard was she had been poisoned and she could die. I phoned Rick but spoke to Keira who seemed sympathetic and promised to let him know.

It was a very long night. I lifted Fleur up onto my bed and stroked her until she fell asleep. I lay awake, my hand buried in her fur, banishing the thought of life without her. The vet said that if the antibiotics did work, I would notice by the next day. I must have slept because I was woken by Fleur, who was pawing my cheek. Instantly alert, I examined her. She didn't seem to have deteriorated in the night, and if anything, seemed a tiny bit better. A feeling of hope and tentative relief made me tearful and raw. I checked to see if Rick had tried to return my call, and he hadn't. I knew in my bones it was the wrong thing to do, but I phoned him again and I'm not sure what I intended to say, but this is what actually happened.

'Hi, it's me Joanie. I thought you might be vaguely interested to know that Fleur is OK now.'

'Why? What was wrong with her?'

'If you'd taken five minutes out of your busy life, you might have phoned to ask!'

Obvious confusion. 'What's up, Joanie?'

'I know you don't care about me, but I hoped you would have cared enough to call me back when I told you Fleur was really ill. She nearly died.'

'I didn't know!'

'Well I told Keira!'

Silence. And then, like a pool of fetid water, all the months of pent up misery rose and ran from me like a river of rage as I raked over the suppurating sore of our breakup. I flung all the hurts I had endured, the feelings of rejection, and self pity-yes, I knew even then it was self pity-right at him. If Rick tried to say anything, to interrupt me on my kamikaze mind dump, I wouldn't have heard. When I'd finally run out of things to say, all could be heard was my breathless silence. I waited a moment before hanging up and then I wept and wept and wept. It felt good.

Over the next two days, Fleur recovered the use of her hind legs and her appetite and as I watched her return to her old self, I felt a similar feeling; a second chance. A return to my old self, the one with confidence who didn't feel like the girl who was left behind, the feeling that I had finally left Rick behind. Perhaps I needed to get everything out of my system before I could move on. So redemption for Fleur and perhaps a new start for me?

❧ ⬙ ✧ ⬙ ❧

Rick disappeared in the early Autumn. He left notes for Keira, Marva, friends, family, even me, and the occasional email would appear, so at least we knew he was alive, but there were concerns for his mental health. Did he have a history of depression? Was he perhaps bipolar, like Stephen Fry when he did a similar thing? If anyone knew where he was, they weren't saying and the media speculation was rife, so Marva let it be known that he was in the States 'finding himself', and writing songs. Keira as the sad girlfriend left behind, attracted a huge wave of publicity that did her career no harm. And me? I felt guilty and concerned. It wasn't like him to do a disappearing act. As the days rolled on concern became worry.

Marva called me and asked if I would meet her at her office. She had a proposal but she didn't want to talk over the phone. My curiosity was whipped to a keen peak as I sat on her low sofa. Lighting up a cigarette, she tottered on her stilettos round her huge desk and lowered herself down to join me.

'Now my darling,' she started, 'you know we're all concerned about Rick! This whole disappearing business...a nightmare! A nightmare! That boy is like a son to me and I haven't had a moment's sleep since he disappeared!' She lay her hand on my arm and searched to gain eye contact as I shrank further into the sofa.

'Did you know?' she continued, 'that since he finished Arc Unfinished, he hasn't written one song, not one? I have torn my hair out, torn it out trying to think of ways to help him. This sensitivity is of course a mark of his genius. He is a genius, you know that don't you? But there is no point being a genius if you keep it all to yourself!'

Rick? A genius? I think not. I raised my eyebrows and tried to formulate a response. No need, as it turned out, because Marva got to her feet and began pacing.

'I know you still care for him. Who wouldn't, a handsome boy like him?' Her pacing slowed and she slid a sidelong glance at me. I remained impassive.

'I know you and I haven't exactly hit it off in the past, but you have to believe me when I say that all I want to do is help him. So last night, I was tossing and turning…you don't want to know how I toss and turn, toss and turn... and then, it came to me! A way to help him to write his beautiful songs again.' She stubbed her cigarette out into the already full ashtray before returning to sit beside me.

'It's you Jane..'

'Joanie'

'Joanie. You are the solution! I can see it as clear as day. You need to find him and inspire him again. Now, you may well ask me what about Keira? Well let me be the first to tell you… it's all over between them! Keira was in here last week sobbing her poor eyes out! She confided in me-they all do, darling- she told me it's all over! He told her before he…disappeared. Something about a dog. Why don't you go get him and bring him home? Then let nature take it's course!'

'Do you know where he is?'

'No, but I have a sneaking suspicion you do.'

I reeled out of Marva's office and took lungfuls of smoke-free air. It occurred to me that in all the time I was there, I had hardly said a thing, except that is, to name my price.

The sun was trying to shine early on the Saturday morning as Fleur and I drove to Pembrokeshire to the cottage we had stayed in with Rick over a year ago. It had belonged to his recently deceased Aunt and was lying empty whilst relatives decided what to do with it. As soon as I reached the wooden gate that crossed the rutted track down to the cottage, I knew he was there. Perhaps he didn't hear the car because he came out of the cottage and was walking fast in the opposite direction. I called him and he turned.

'Joanie!'

'I knew you'd be here...'

Fleur, released from the car, was running wild circles and barking her excitement. He threw his arm over my shoulder and hauled me into the cottage, whistling for Fleur to follow.

'Marva's in a funk' I remarked as we settled down with a cup of tea, 'says you haven't written any music since Arc.'

'Obviously not.'

'So, what are you going to do about it?'

'Joanie?'

I looked him in the eye 'It's not going to happen Rick. We're over.'

'I know. But you know how it is.'

I slumped back in the faded chintz armchair and considered the situation. 'This time, I want a contract.'

'Done.' I grabbed his guitar and began doing what I have always done. I started on our next song.

The Meaning of Love

Jackie Vickers

'I just think it's time she settled down, Jack. With the right man, of course.' I didn't expect a reply, he never does say much.

Linda moved back from London a couple of years ago. She lives at the other end of our town, it's only a little terrace house but it's enough for one. I like to go and tidy up for her - just the kitchen and living room - and do her ironing. Only she seems to have company, of one sort or another, most of the time. Jack says I should leave her to get on with her life. I say it's natural for mothers to lend a hand.

'It might be natural for a daughter to want her independence, especially at thirty.' Then he stamps off to cut the grass. All these years and he still gives me the silent treatment. Last week I went round to Linda's, as per usual, and got the shock of my life. I'd just started on the kitchen, which was in a worse state than ever, when I heard the living room door open.

'I wasn't expecting the cleaner. I'm afraid I've taken over the sitting room.' A big fella stood in the doorway and behind him I could see there were books and papers scattered all over the floor.

'I'm not the cleaner, I'm Linda's mother! I always come Wednesdays.'

'Ah,' he said. 'Well, I do have rather a lot to do. Couldn't you come back this afternoon?'

He was from the university, he said, but he looked more like a bouncer. A bald bouncer at that.

Jack was trimming the hedge when I got back.

'Switch that thing off, I've got something to tell you. Linda's got a new man.'

'She's always got a new man.' Jack switched the strimmer back on, so that put paid to any conversation.

Then, at long last, she gets someone special. He must be special, because she asks to bring him round for a roast dinner on Sunday.

Linda wanted Yorkshire Pudding. 'Max is mad about everything Yorkshire.'

'At least he's not a vegetarian then,' I said to Jack. When Aidan lived with her we went round for a meal, just the once. Linda's not much of a cook and I have to say it showed.

Though Jack said, 'perhaps it's supposed to taste like that'.

I haven't got my hopes up, though, with this new fella. You never know with Linda. Though Max is better looking than her previous boyfriends, plus a good head of hair on him, and I will say he has good ideas. He had plans for her back garden, even though it's only a tiny plot.

'Decking is what we need!' They got all the wood, but he was held up at work, so Jack finished it off for them. It's a bit green and slimy now, they never did get round to those barbecues.

'It was never going to work, a north-facing plot, always in the shade.' Jack said.

'Give the chap credit for having some vision. How was Max to know it would rain all summer?' He had no answer to that.

Max had another good idea. One weekend he sent Linda off with her best friend Tiffany and set about painting her sitting room as a surprise. He thought a bright yellow (citrus he called it) would liven things up. Only he got a bit behind and asked Jack if he would help. I still say Jack shouldn't have told him yellow was the one colour Linda can't abide. Having to cover it with magnolia put the whole business even more behind. I think the trouble between them started there.

'Well it is her house,' said Jack.

'You have to keep a still tongue in your head sometimes,' I told him. 'For the sake of the relationship,' I explained. He didn't get the point and went off somewhere in the car.

Soon after the painting fiasco, Linda called to say I shouldn't come over Wednesdays as they're getting a dog.

'Good idea,' says Jack.

'Noisy, smelly things, if you ask me. And it'll put a damper on their lifestyle.'

'If it puts a damper on his DIY activities, that'll be something.'

I did a roast as usual on Sunday but Linda came on her own.

'Max said he couldn't bring the puppy, it might chew things.'

I thought they could have left it for an hour or two but apparently you can't leave puppies. Or not this one. A few days later, I bumped into Linda at her Co-op, buying dog food. Tiffany was with her, wobbling about on some smart red strappy contraptions. I must say she makes something of herself.

'How's Max?'

'Very tired. He works most evenings now.'

That dog'll be wearing her out, I told Jack later. I described what Linda was wearing and how smart Tiffany was, but when I looked up he'd gone to sleep.

Eventually they reckoned the dog - they call him Caesar - knew me well enough to be able to cope with my cleaning. Either that, or the place got so bad they couldn't stand it. Caesar was fully grown now and big, being a Labrador. He was cooped up in that tiny kitchen, so I let him out into the living room. He ran straight behind the couch, sniffing and growling and pawing at a holdall. I tried to pull him away but he had his head in it. They were Max's things so I thought 'let him'. He should put his things away. Then Caesar gives a yelp and pulls something out and starts chewing. He's not a puppy any more but still he chews. Not properly trained you see. I pulled the couch out to get round Caesar and there it was. A red shoe with the highest heels I've ever seen and straps and laces hanging from the sole, the sort of shoe that men notice. The sort of shoe Tiffany was wearing in town that day. I grabbed at it and the dog growled, slavering all over it, bits of red strap on the carpet. He held it down with his paws and tore at it the way you see lions eating their prey. Nasty with it, too, wouldn't let me near. Then I heard the key in the lock.

Linda stared at the remains of the shoe, white-faced.

'I'll make you a cup of tea.' I said.

'No thanks. I've got things to do.'

'What does she mean, I've got things to do? Kill Max? Kill the dog?'

'Your lurid imagination,' said Jack. 'I hope she gets rid of the useless article.' He wouldn't talk about it and went off in the car leaving me with my heart thumping.

At long last I heard him come back and met him at the door. 'How is she?' Because if I don't ask he'll never say.

'She reckons she's found the meaning of love,' Jack says, looking pleased with himself. 'So, all's well that ends well, and they're coming for dinner on Sunday.'

'What a relief. I'll make an apple pie.'

Jack gave me a funny look. 'I don't think Caesar likes apple pie.'

Feline Friendship

Wendy Greenberg

Night on the Tiles

We are going out.
Me, rhinestones and red velvet
You, glossy black fur

Look…no greys…

A full bodywash
I preen to a sleek silky shine
Because I'm worth it

Delightful dotage

I talk you listen
We're growing old together
Purring and dozing

Home Improvements

We built our kitchen
Around the cat flap access
You think I'm joking?

A Little Unpleasantness

Andrew Bax

S low down Roger – you'll startle that horse.'

'Oh no!' Roger exclaimed in mock horror. 'It's Miss Armstrong – as if I won't be seeing enough of her tonight.'

'Now don't be silly, Roger. A bit of culture will do you good. I don't think she knows we're here,' Penny added absently.

Roger changed down into second gear and glared at the substantial rump ahead. Miss Armstrong and her enormous gelding, Saracen, had been together for as long as anyone could remember. So long, in fact, that they had started to look alike. Whether it was Saracen who changed to look like Miss Armstrong, or the other way about, was a common topic for conjecture in the village. She lived in a crumbling old manor house with a meek, bald-headed little man who played the organ in church. The precise nature of their relationship was another topic for conjecture in the village.

'Why doesn't the blasted woman turn into that gateway and let us by?'

'Now calm down Roger – I want you on your best behaviour tonight.' Penny Cartwright, chairperson of the Village Hall Committee had been planning the concert for months. It was almost sold out, mainly because she had found a part for all the children in the school, guaranteeing an audience of parents. But Miss Armstrong was her star turn.

'Tough as old boots and twice as ugly,' was Roger's reaction.

With thoughts on her forthcoming excerpts from the Sound of Music, Miss Armstrong was oblivious to the frustration she was causing. Saracen knew every inch of these narrow lanes and when pointed in the direction of home, could be guaranteed to get her there unaided. He clip-clopped steadily on but then, suddenly, he stopped dead. Miss Armstrong awoke from her reverie and tried to urge Saracen on with a few gentle digs into his massive flanks. Harder digs had no effect; neither did a tap with her riding crop. But a car horn, blown right behind him, certainly did.

All sixteen hands of Saracen reared high into the air with Miss Armstrong making frantic efforts to grab him round the neck; then he bucked, kicking his vast hooves only inches from the Cartwright's windscreen. A few skittish sideways moves – and he was off, galloping down the lane with Miss Armstrong, having lost her stirrups, reins and dignity, but still clinging on.

In the Cartwright's car there was silence. Then Penny spoke: 'Are you alright Roger?'

'I thought he was going to land on top of us.' Roger sounded shaken.

'So did I. I was really frightened.'

'Maybe it wasn't a good idea to blow the horn.'

'No – I don't think it was.'

'Did she see us – Miss Armstrong I mean?'

'I don't think so. Perhaps we shouldn't say anything about it.'

'Good idea.' Roger turned the car round and drove home another way.

In the meantime Saracen, with Miss Armstrong still loosely connected, had crashed through a hedge into a field of sheep. After a couple of circuits, scattering sheep in all directions, he slowed to a trot, and then stopped to look about him. Only then did an exhausted Miss Armstrong loosen her grip and slide off in a heap.

The Cartwrights did not normally drink at lunchtime but, they decided, this morning's events called for a restorative bottle of Rioja. When the telephone rang, Penny answered: 'Miss Armstrong! How are you? ... No! How frightful! Are you alright? ... Those lads from the estate I expect ... The police! Are you sure that's necessary? ... You're quite sure you will be alright for tonight? ... Roger was only saying how tough you are ... You really are a brick. The show must go on!' Thinking that Miss Armstrong had been mollified, they opened another bottle.

But Miss Armstrong was far from mollified. She had expected Penny to give her more support in finding the perpetrator of the morning's outrage, and she didn't like being called a brick. So when all those involved gathered at the village hall before the concert was due to begin, there was an unsettling tension backstage.

'Ah Penny, there you are!' exclaimed Miss Armstrong 'I was just telling Derek Manners here about my nasty experience – and he said, didn't you Derek? – that perhaps you should ask for witnesses from the stage, Penny.'

'Miss Armstrong thinks she may have seen a small silver car,' said Derek, with a wink.

'But what good would that do? It was probably a mistake and everyone I've been talking to thinks you're a real brick to carry on. It would only spoil things if you made a scene about it now.'

'I am not a brick and I am not making a scene,' wailed Miss Armstrong, close to tears. 'Tell her, Derek.' But Derek, billed tonight as Blue Suede Shoes, was nowhere to be seen.

There were calls for quiet as the choir prepared to go on stage. 'Shhhh,' said Penny.

'Don't shush me!' retorted the evening's star, really upset now. She looked terrible.

'Now we don't want any unpleasantness. Think of the children.'

'I *am* thinking of the children. They may have seen something.'

'They think you are a hero. Don't spoil it for them.' But Miss Armstrong did not want to be a hero; she wanted retribution. Anxious people fussed about her and she sank into a chair, sensing defeat.

'I can't go on,' she whimpered, but no-one took any notice. Instead they agreed that she was wonderful. Someone produced some vodka; someone else found and cleaned a jam jar left over from the afternoon's Over 60's art class. Miss Armstrong, who had never tasted vodka before, took a sip.

In the meantime the school choir was generating such a happy atmosphere with the audience that the other acts were certain to be received with rapturous applause, unless they were truly awful. Unfortunately, the local folk group which was on next, *was* truly awful and Penny, fearing a walk-out, marched on stage clapping and smiling, but telling them to clear off.

Then it was Blue Suede Shoes. Derek Manners whose van, hand-painted The Maintenance Man, was a familiar and popular figure in the village. He knew the eccentric plumbing in all the older houses and unwittingly added a few twists of his own; no recent regulation guided his electrical connections; and he lacked the eye to make a course of bricks run straight – but everything seemed to work. However, as Banford

Dingley's very own Elvis impersonator, he was – well, laughable.

His arrival on stage was greeted with facetious cheers – and the applause was even louder when he finished. Some wags in the audience kept it going far longer than was necessary but, to everyone's relief, Derek did not respond to the calls for an encore.

During the interval he came up to Roger. 'A word in your ear, Mr Cartwright, if you have a moment.'

'Hello Derek. Wonderful performance – I particularly enjoyed *Its Now or Never*.'

'Thank you Mr Cartwright. I just thought you should know, like. I saw it all – I was right behind you.'

'What? When?'

'This morning. That horse bolting off with Miss Armstrong.' Roger went rigid.

'Don't worry,' Derek continued 'I won't say anything. But about that gatepost. I've straightened it out now, so let's call it cash – tomorrow.' And with a wink that looked more like a leer he disappeared into the crowd.

Backstage, Miss Armstrong was becoming loud and personal. She decided she disliked everyone around her; in particular she disliked Penny Cartwright who hadn't been in the village more than ten years and had already wormed her way into the Parish Council and everything else. Everything annoyed her: although it had seen action in many a hunt ball she suddenly felt ridiculous in her ancient bridesmaid's dress, and she was sick and tired of *The Sound of Music*. She reached for the jam jar and considered her options. She could walk out now and let them stew; she could go on stage, denounce imbecile drivers and pushy new-comers and *then* walk out; or ... but her resolve seemed to weaken with every sip. With a heavy sigh, she reached a decision.

'Where's that bald-headed little man?' she called out. Without waiting for an answer she hauled herself up, pushed some loose hair from her face and strode, a little unsteadily, towards the stage.

The interval was over and a frazzled Penny was struggling with what to tell the audience. Miss Armstrong had been downright offensive, frankly, and the way she had been waving that jam jar about – well, it was a disgrace. And besides, she had said she was not going on; she had made that *very* clear.

'Ladies and gentlemen,' she began 'I'm afraid there has been a bit of a hitch. Miss Armstrong had a most unfortunate riding accident this morning that has left her rather shaken. All the children have worked so hard in rehearsals and we mustn't let them down, so we will just carry on ... somehow,' she added limply. Penny was going to say quite a lot more about the children when a blur of pink chiffon swept behind her.

'*The hills are alive with the sound of music.*' Miss Armstrong, fuelled on vodka and determination, was in full voice - '*With songs they have sung for a thousand years.*'

Following her, the bald-headed little man darted for the piano; the audience cheered wildly and Penny slid off into the wings, unnoticed. When the applause died down, Miss Armstrong launched into *Do-Re-Mi* with an enthusiastic chorus of school children. 'Such a professional,' the audience agreed 'and after what she's gone through.'

The Lonely Goatherd and *My Favourite Things* followed. Next, she made an unprogrammed diversion into *The King and I* with *Whistle a Happy Tune* calling on the audience to whistle the chorus, but with mixed success because it is impossible to whistle and laugh at the same time – try it yourself. Order was restored with *Sixteen Going on Seventeen*.

The concert was brought to a close with Miss Armstrong and the children leading the audience in a tumultuous rendering of *Edelweiss*. Everyone linked arms and swayed in time with the music, and there wasn't a dry eye in the house. It was a triumph; the little unpleasantness had been forgotten and, not for the first time, Roger felt rather proud of his wife. His satisfaction was marred only by Derek's sudden appearance on the way out – looking rather like a gargoyle Roger thought – to give him another of his leery winks.

Buckland and the Elephant

Ann Edwards

A handbill found crumpled on the floor of the Eagle and Child:

Bostock and Wombwell's Beast Show

Amongst the Number of Natural Curiosities arrived in this City, there seems none to equal or rival the wonderful elephant Esmerelda. Those Ladies and Gentlemen who have already seen this extraordinary pachyderm, are so highly gratified with the sight, that the Proprietor flatters himself, from their high recommendation, that all ranks of people will gratify their curiosity, as she is undoubtedly the only one of her kind ever exhibited in the kingdom alive.

To be seen at St Giles Fair, St Giles Oxford September 1, 1845

'Roll up, roll up. For only three pence you can see her enormous ears, gaze into her ancient eyes and for an extra penny you can feed her a bun. Imagine, ladies and gentlemen, the sensation of her trunk as she takes the bun from your fingers. Dare you sir?'

Mr Bostock, the joint owner of Bostock and Wombwell's Beast Show, was working the crowd. Inside the stiflingly hot canvas awning, Esmerelda the elephant swayed from side to side. The crowd queued patiently, waiting to be ushered in for their audience with the animal. The canvas flaps were lifted and they moved into the gloom of the tent.

'Cor she stinks. Take a whiff of that, Ma,' shrieked a small ginger-haired boy as Esmerelda lifted her tail and defecated.

'That's a massive one. Your dad would only need one of those for the whole allotment,' observed the child's mother.

'Go on then, mate. I'll give you a penny to feed it,' shouted a young man egged on to bravery by his girlfriend.

The elephant raised her sad eyes and with infinite gentleness took the bun from his outstretched hand. She waved the bun above the heads of the crowd before twisting her trunk and popping the bun into her mouth. The crowd roared with laughter.

'Me next, me next,' called the ginger-haired boy, elbowing his way to the front of the bun queue.

The Very Reverend William Buckland, Canon of Christ Church observed to his wife that he had rung three times and no tea had yet arrived.

'It's that blasted fair,' she replied. 'The maid has the day off to go gallivanting. I'll fetch your tea.' She stumbled over the tortoise as she left the room.

Dr Buckland's study contained almost as many live specimens as dead ones. The tortoise lived under the sideboard. A ring-necked parakeet sat on a stand by the window. A gecko rolled its eyes from a glass tank. Every surface of Buckland's study was covered in shells, bones, fossils, minerals, stones, books and half eaten bits of toast. In the centre of this organised chaos sat Dr Buckland with an enormous ginger cat on his knee. His black ecclesiastical robes gave him the appearance of a necromancer. He rubbed the cat affectionately under the chin and it blinked its green eyes at him in appreciation.

'The fair,' he mused to the cat, 'I haven't been for years. I think I would like to go.' The cat feigned interest then looked disgruntled as it was pitched off his knee.

Dr Buckland was a zoophagist. His ambition was to eat his way, for scientific research, through the animal kingdom. While younger men were arguing about Darwin's new theories of evolution, Buckland was eating his way through bluebottles, crocodiles, moles, bats, beetles.

He had started his hobby by trying to eat his way through the animal world in alphabetical order. When aardvark proved too difficult to source he decided to eat what came available and simply to chart his progress through the different species, sub-species and genera, with tasting notes. His rooms in Christ Church were decorated with the skeletal remains of his most interesting meals, mounted in life-like poses.

'We'll move her after dark,' said Mr Bostock. 'I don't want no-one getting a look at her for free'.

The elephant's chain was unbolted from its stake and with sharp pokes behind her ears to encourage her, she was walked across the town to the Christ Church meadows where the rest of the Beast Show was camped. The animal moved slowly and shook her head from side to side.

'She don't look well, Boss' said one of the costermongers.

A jet of green, stinking faeces exploded from her and spattered all over Mr Bostock's trousers.

'Shit' he said.

As the sun rose over the Isis and the mist of morning evaporated away, Esmerelda the elephant died.

Dr Buckland whistled as he walked to the Beast Show camp. The rat tucked inside his hassock fidgeted and stuck its nose out of the vestments to see where they were. 'Stop that! It tickles,' The Very Reverend remonstrated. 'Excuse me young man, I would like to see the elephant.'

'Miss, if you don't mind' said Consuela, the Bearded Lady, 'Better ask the boss, that's him over there. I don't know how much he's going to charge to see a dead one. Can't imagine there's going to be much demand myself.'

Buckland's heart missed a beat.

'Dead?' He almost sprinted over to Mr Bostock. 'When did it die?' he asked.

'Bloody hell. Have you come to give it the Last Rites?' said Mr Bostock.

'No, no, no. I would like to buy the carcass,' said Buckland.

Mr Bostock stopped looking depressed and started to look shifty.

'Well, that's a very valuable bit of meat, that is. How much is it worth to you?'

Buckland threw caution to the wind and said with great aplomb 'Three shillings and six pence.'

'You are taking the mickey, Reverend. I could feed the lions for a month on Esmerelda. I need at least ten guineas to make it worth my while.'

'I'll pay you eleven including delivery' said Buckland, who was warming to the art of negotiation.

There was a tricky moment as they negotiated the gate into Tom Quad in Christ Church College, but with a lot of shoving and pushing, the late Esmerelda eventually popped like a cork out of a bottle on to the grass.

Now Buckland had his elephant, how was he to cook it? His scientific mind turned hypotheses and parameters, paradigms and conjectures till his synapses ached. If he was successful who would remember Darwin with his ridiculous new ideas? It would be Buckland's name that would echo down the ages. Cheered by this thought he set to work. So what to do? He wrote and drew till the cat, thoroughly exasperated, got off his knee and went to sit on its own, throwing him the occasional dirty look.

a. He could joint the carcass and cook it in pieces, but no, he knew the college butcher – Mr Grimshaw wouldn't have a chopper big enough.

b. He could wrap it in pastry. Elephant pie. He didn't like pie.

c. He could cover it in breadcrumbs. He didn't have a dish big enough to roll it in.

Buckland was beginning to feel dispirited.

'You could roast it' his wife suggested bringing him more tea and toast, 'but you will have to keep the meat moist. You don't want it to be tough. If I was you I'd stuff it.'

'What will I stuff it with?'

'Pigs' said Mrs Buckland, who was a resourceful and imaginative cook, 'and then you would have some extra meat in case there wasn't enough to go round.'

Buckland worked for two days non-stop until he had finished the masterpiece of his later life 'How to cook an elephant.' Extracts of which now follow:

- Dig a pit twelve feet square and eight feet deep (in the middle of Tom Quad).

- Construct tunnels at each corner to act as chimneys with a turn spit/bellows arrangement at each tunnel mouth.

- Line bottom and sides with three feet of charcoal.

- Light charcoal with small pastilles. Insert prepared and oven-ready elephant.

- Pour gravel and top soil over elephant to seal

- Keep fanning until the temperature reaches two hundred degrees Fahrenheit

- Cook for the required time and serve.

In calculating the cooking time, (thirty one and a half hours), Buckland took the bold decision to ignore heat losses through the earth, including the sides and ends of the pit. He reasoned that heat would be conducted through the meat and it would heat up until a state of equilibrium was reached, with as much heat being conducted through the meat as is lost to the earth, atmosphere etc. If the fire failed it might be possible that there would be insufficient heat to maintain the temperature of the meat at an adequate level but, he reasoned, some people may like their elephant rare. *Quod est demonstrandum*, his feast would be ready on Thursday at seven pm.

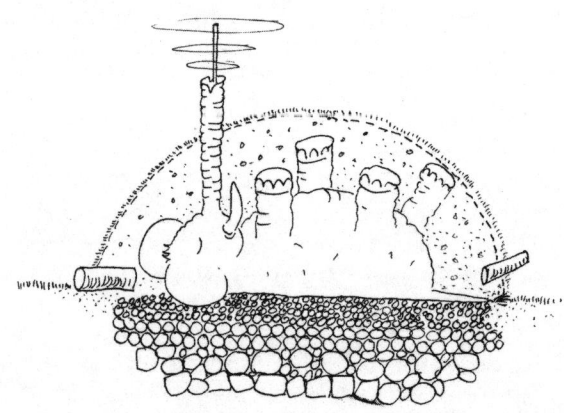

Buckland, confident that his science would work, retired to bed.

'I'd like to see the look on Darwin's face when he hears about this,' he thought as sleep possessed him.

After morning prayers, Buckland, with a supportive audience of Canons leaning from the windows of Tom Quad, prepared for the mammoth task ahead of him. With the animal lying on her side, he slowly paced across to the furthest wall of the quad, turned and, armed with a pike-staff, ran like the clappers towards the beast. There was a loud pop, as the pike-staff punctured Esmerelda's stomach and she started to deflate like a balloon. There was a hiss as her intestinal gases started to escape and moments later a torrent of blood sprayed out of the wound, covering Dr Buckland from head to toe.

'I was not expecting that,' he told his appreciative audience.

Esmerelda's now flaccid belly was supported by two of the strongest kitchen porters. Buckland, still dripping blood, slit her from front to back and then poked a small scullery boy into the opening with the injunction to hold his nose. The boy, who was known universally afterwards as Stinker, rummaged around inside the carcass throwing out the vital organs to Buckland's waiting arms.

To Buckland's satisfaction, he managed to stretch her intestines all around the quad perimeter and passing students had to step daintily over them. A pack of fox hounds appeared and were keen to help. Their baying and howling, the gagging noises from Stinker as he emerged from the carcass and the buzz of the thousands of bluebottles all contributed to the carnival atmosphere.

When Dr Buckland opened Esmerelda's stomach he was interested to find an inordinate quantity of half-digested buns, one pound, seven and sixpence in small change, and a bunch of keys. He made a mental note to return the keys to Mr Bostock. The college cooks stepped forward. Esmerelda was stuffed with three pigs, each pig stuffed with a capon and each capon stuffed with sweet bay leaves, and the cavity was sewn shut. Ropes were attached front and back.

Buckland arranged his work-force into two teams. One team was to balance the animal, while the other team was to move her into the pit or 'Elephantarium fornax' as it was now called. After much heaving the elephant was rolled into her final resting place.

Esmerelda was cooked lying on her back with her legs in the air and with the tip of her trunk sticking out of the oven to act as a pie funnel.

The fire burnt, the elephant cooked, the smell of roasting meat filled Oxford. An interested crowd gathered at the gate to the quad and jostled to peer in. The dons stood around occasionally fanning the flames with their gowns. The undergraduates larked about and the Very Reverend Buckland sharpened his carving knife.

As the bell, Big Tom, brother to the more famous Ben, struck seven, the pit was opened and the elephant was revealed. The cooks tied ropes around her legs and dragged her up onto the remnants of the lawns where they started to carve her.

In Christ Church's ancient dining hall the tables were laid for the feast. The college silver and crystal glinted in the candlelight. The blue-faced gargoyles stuck their red tongues out rudely at the proceedings. The only woman at the feast was Elizabeth I who looked down from her portrait hung above the High Table. She would have enjoyed the event, having the stomach of a king. The doors opened and in staggered the college porters carrying trestle tables loaded with mountains of meat. The meat itself was a rather alarming red. At the lectern, to the side of the top-table, Buckland stood to read the Horace-inspired epigram he had composed in place of the normal College grace:

Nunc est bibendum, nunc pede libero barrus pulsanda tellus.

This translates as 'Now is the time for drinking, now is the time to beat the earth with unfettered elephants' feet'.

Esmerelda fed three hundred people, with enough leftovers to keep the workhouse in broth for a month. Buckland was the first to be served. He piled his plate high as an encouragement to the others. He selected for himself the animal's tail as a particular delicacy. Esmerelda's trunk, a little charred on the outside, was carved into pretty rings, like calamari. He had one of those as well. Cumberland sauce was served as an accompaniment. He had thought long and hard as to what beverages should accompany the meal. In the stygian darkness of the college wine cellar he had come across a box labelled 'Ritual Siberian Shaman Elixir.' This substance is made by Siberian shamans, who consume large quantities of the hallucinogenic fly agaric mushroom. The tribe, wanting to share in the shaman's experience, then drink his urine. These samples had been donated to the college in 1837 by Colonel FFyensTodgerington after his wife had mistakenly opened a bottle and given it to her bridge ladies.

'Just the thing' he said.

As the dark brown viscous liquid was poured into the masters' glasses the students looked quietly relieved that, through college funding cuts, they were limited to beer. It took the party nearly five hours to consume the meal. And what did it taste like? It was agreed by most people that it was an acquired taste. Buckland thought it tasted like crocodile.

Also published in Imagine Oxford edited by Jackie Vickers

The Brewhouse Cats

Nichola May

As Margaret ripped off the final piece of parcel tape with a careless *whoop*, the slit of the box sprung open and she dived in. She emerged with small pieces of broken polystyrene hanging from her mousy perm and released the shrink-wrapped package with a pair of embroidery scissors.

This latest purchase had been a personal recommendation from Sandy. 'I got just a ting for your troubles Mrs Anderson,' Sandy said after the second cup of tea. 'You the only one of my ladies who hasn't bought one.'

Last month 'just a ting' had been the everlasting nylon carpet anti-static device; the previous month it had been the tropical spider-displacer; and before then the simple pimple-extractor, the all-purpose metal handle degreaser, the ready-steady anyway-up household glove, and the under-shelf handy bottle-top storage compartment. Margaret had lost count of all the objects that had been 'just a ting' for her troubles.

'This catalogue is the modern solution for the busy woman,' Sandy said. 'It is time, Mrs Anderson, for us women to rise up from our domestic chains and be free as the cat on the roofs.'

Sandy first appeared in Paradise Square on a gloomy Tuesday back in February. Margaret had been halfway through a documentary about bubble-wrap, when she was interrupted by her *50-in-1 tunes* door bell. She opened the door to find a woman on the doorstep. The woman's shiny face was wound into a headscarf of such bright colours it looked as if she had been wrapped in a bunch of dahlias.

'My name,' the woman announced, 'is Sanura Butama. But my friends call me Sandy.' And with that, a gust of wind inflated her unbuttoned coat and blew her into the hallway.

Sandy's musical voice swept through the house like waves on a tropical beach. Her hair, once released from the confines of the head scarf, took flight in twirls of delight as if dancing to some prohibited beat all of its own. Sandy's catalogue, full of items that Margaret had never seen or needed before, was irresistible.

The cat-scarer was bigger than Margaret expected. It was not, as she remembered from the catalogue, a sitting down cat. No. This was a ready-to-pounce cat. It had two green translucent jewels for eyes and something at the back that resembled a battery pack.

But where to put it? None of the houses in Paradise Square had a back garden. Margaret removed the broken *Santa Stop Here* sign from the planter by the front door and replaced it with the spike of the cat-scarer.

'What on earth do we want with that?' Kenneth said in bed that night.

'Everyone has one,' Margaret said. 'I thought you might be pleased.'

But Kenneth wasn't pleased. Kenneth was rarely pleased about anything. He brushed the biscuit crumbs across the bedcover straight onto Margaret's side. Margaret made a mental note to buy a hand-held mini vac from next month's catalogue.

From her bedroom window Margaret could see along most of Paradise Square, which wasn't really a square at all, but rather an L-shaped road, sandwiched between two pubs and a tumble of garish red-brick flats built on the site where the brewery once was. The chimney of the brewhouse remained, but was trapped like some ancient relic inside a courtyard of flats. Another relic, the old brewery gate, gave the flats a deceptively grand entrance.

Most of Margaret's neighbours had bought a cat-scarer. The family next door to Margaret, an oriental-looking lady with four pretty daughters, had placed a cat-scarer on their front lawn. It was the only lawn on Paradise Square.

The grey-haired arthritic Mrs Ballentino at no. 84 had placed a cat-scarer between her collection of ornamental hedgehogs and a cement rabbit.

'Indicative of the lower classes,' Kenneth said.

At the rental house, no. 78, one of the students with long ginger hair and piercings had climbed out of a top window and fixed a cat-scarer on the roof like a weather vane. Kenneth phoned the planning office to complain.

That evening Margaret went to bed as usual, but a terse discussion with Kenneth about eating biscuits in bed left her irritated and restless. The night was humid. The net curtains, sucked in and out of the open bedroom window on imaginary air, brought with them stagnant sounds from the street below.

In the early hours when the heat was at its greatest, something startled her. She listened. It was a sound she didn't recognise. Margaret slipped out from under the covers, stepped into her fawn slippers and white housecoat and went downstairs. She stood at the front doorstep, fanning herself with July's catalogue supplement. She wished she'd bought those Cool Air System Lounging Shoes.

She heard the noise again. As she looked down, Margaret saw that there was a cat sitting at the bottom of her steps. The cat stood up, wound itself between her legs and gave out a sorrowful cry.

The cat followed her into the kitchen. It looked hungry. Margaret took out the salmon she had set aside for Kenneth's supper.

'Well he can just do without, can't he?' she said, scraping the fish into a china bowl and placing it on the front step. While the cat ate Kenneth's meal, Margaret examined it. She reached towards its collar to see if there was name tag. It was then that Margaret saw it!

Suspended on a ribbon from the cat's collar, and wrapped in almost translucent tissue paper, was a tiny box-shaped package. The corners were folded with such precision that it could have been wrapped by elves. Margaret ran her tongue along her lips and gently moved her hand towards the collar. The cat retreated with a yowl. Tail high and without looking back, it trotted into the darkness.

The following day Margaret spent over an hour looking around Paradise Square, but there was no sign of the cat. Hoping it might return in the evening, she ordered a crate of *Supreme Cat Food* and *Purrfect Nibbles*. She hummed to herself as she arranged the tins at the back of the cupboard where Kenneth wouldn't see them.

In the evening, Margaret listened and watched. Late in the evening she heard its pitiful miaows at the door. She found it sat on the doorstep, its fur flattened with rain. The package, however, was as dry and perfect as the first evening Margaret had spotted it.

Margaret presented the cat with a bowl of the most expensive cat food and waited patiently. When there was nothing left but the soft crumbs of food on the cat's whiskers Margaret crept forward as if to stroke, then lunged. The cat leapt back with a screech. Its fur sprung into a mohican down the ridges of its spine, and it took flight into the darkness.

Desperate and enraged, Margaret hitched up her housecoat with both hands and flung herself down the street. Her fawn slippers slapped the tarmac at high speed, her fat knees tumbled past each other and the wild tail of her housecoat cord flew out behind her. At the end of Paradise Square Margaret's smooth soles lost grip and she slid, nearly tumbling into the weir.

She saw the cat's reflective eyes taunting her from the end of Quaking Bridge and set off again in pursuit. The cat sped past the pub, down St Thomas' Street, turned its head then scampered down an entrance towards the flats.

'No!' Margaret sobbed. 'No! I will get you!' She took a sharp left after the cat and then skidded to a stop.

In the courtyard, beyond the brewery gate, thirty pairs of eyes, or maybe more, were staring out at her. Moving. Blinking in synchronization. As if from one huge creature. There was not one cat, but many cats.

Margaret stepped under the ironwork arch of the brewery gate and through into the courtyard. There were cats of all sizes and types; a tiny Siamese-type cat with four pretty little kittens, a grey-haired cat with arthritic legs, a long-haired ginger cat with a spiky studded collar, and many more besides.

But the only cat Margaret was interested in was *her* cat, the cat with the perfect little package. It watched her. She approached it. Her heart beating with anticipation, she crouched down and ever-so-slowly slipped the package from its collar.

Margaret took the tiny box between finger and thumb. The sound of the millstream was roaring through her head. The cat watched her as she cupped the package in her hand, and then, barely breathing, she tugged at the ribbon. It came away in her hand so easily, so perfectly.

The sheet of tissue paper released, melted into the rain, and the contents rolled into Margaret's palm. Her housecoat tail twitched. Then her lips parted and she let out a purr of delight.

When Kenneth woke up the next morning he was furious. His clothes weren't laid out for him, there was no breakfast, and instead of his nicely prepared lunchbox there were empty tins of cat food littering the draining board. He grabbed his coat and marched out of the door, knocking an empty bowl off the doorstep.

In the bedroom the morning sun was trying to break through a gap in the almost-closed curtains. A flicker of light bounced off the wall. Where it rested it illuminated a patch on the bed, where a white cat with fawn paws was licking biscuit crumbs from the covers.

You Can't Get the Staff

Wendy Greenberg

'What's not to like?' was the opening gambit from the salesman '...smart technology at its best. You, the customer, really in control. Once we install the equipment you can use this app on your Smartphone to monitor the power usage in your home; turn thermostats down remotely; switch off, or of course on, when your daily schedule changes and all in all really keep control of your heating bills. We guarantee that you will feel in charge, Mr Walker' he nodded his head, 'and you will immediately notice the results in your bills... It's a win/win.'

'Win/win? Really?' said Denise. The gas man turned, as if noticing her for the first time.

'I promise you Mrs Walker, that, when you see how often you are heating an empty house, you will turn the heating off. With the savings you make there will be more money for other things.'

'So we can both use the technology can we?'

'The application will be available to the bill holder.'

Monty smirked, shook the salesman's hand and asked where he should sign. Ralph curled up on the sofa cushion and closed his eyes.

It was only yesterday that Ralph's sleep was disturbed by bickering voices. He adjusted his position, legs akimbo in the late afternoon sunshine. It was difficult not to listen and he was irritated, all over again, by his inability to choose the right staff. His need for quiet repose should surely mean their problems should be taken below stairs. They were really going for it today, something about smart technology which, naturally, was of absolutely no interest to him. He shut his eyes and feigned sleep – his usual approach to staff disputes. But Ralph could not settle and, as he picked up the words 'central heating', he reluctantly opened one eye, stretched and swung towards the source of the problem.

'I tell you Monty, I'm not having it.'

'Don't start telling me what we're having, or not having – it could save us hundreds, thousands even.'

'It could…granted… if we use less.'

'Precisely, my darling.'

'No...Monty...don't darling me, it is NOT going to happen.'

On and on they went Ralph could not believe that experienced staff could behave like this. They must know that an easy-going, warm ambience was the key to his wellbeing. He had specifically short-listed all his candidates on the basis of their skills in this department, his tail quivered as he heard Denise's parting salvo:

'and, of course we need to think about Ralph...'

There was no doubt about the sincerity of Denise's message as it was backed up by an explosive crash, shaking the old door on its insecure hinges. The reverberations and the following icy draught bounced through Ralph's bones, every nerve shaken to attention. These were bad vibrations, but did demonstrate he hadn't got the selection process completely wrong. He would, however, have to address the Monty problem. The issue was underlined as Monty continued shouting at an absent Denise.

'Ralph? Ralph is here on his own...with every radiator in the house pumping out heat, so that the house is just perfect for him and like the tropics when you come home. I rest my case.'

Ralph wound himself round Denise's legs. He hated this play acting but some way of pointing out the current lapses in the schedule was necessary. He stared at his dish which, he noted, was empty again. The housekeeping was suffering too, never a good sign.

'RALPH IS NOT ON HIS OWN - had you forgotten that I can work from home'

Ralph didn't like change and the omens were not good. In the last resort he could move again but he didn't fancy practising the necessary fawning routine when he would much rather stay put. Hiring and firing was such a bore. He slunk up the stairs and settled into one of his favourite spots across the top step where the heating system ran closely under the floorboards and, whilst organising his thoughts, dozed off.

Ralph adapted to his altered circumstances with distaste, He shared his displeasure by increasing the chores required of his housekeepers. He abandoned the narrow hole in the door designed for him to access the outside, choosing instead a more personal door service from his staff. He found an alternative heat source in the compost heap along the road then came home to relax on the counter top leaving paw prints on the black granite surface. He even had several sessions chewing the long grass from next door's 'wildlife area', clearing his palate afterwards by spitting the greenery across the kitchen floor.

With the new routine in place, Ralph clocked Monty bouncing off to work each day with a misplaced sense of self-worth as Head of the Household. What was worse was that his Chief of Staff, Denise, began to drift back to her office rather than linger at home. Ralph knew that it was down to him to save the situation for both Denise & himself. Monty was bad news. As if he needed any reminder the pipes clanked and the house shivered.

Ralph slumped around with increasing irritation. He had found a way into the forbidden airing cupboard, spending most mornings mulling over the possibilities whilst moulting and practising his claw skills in the white towel corner. He spent his afternoons trying to establish what a thermostat was and where the central heating controls might be.

When they came home, the heating followed but the conflict continued to be aired in their shared living space.

'Denise…we need to talk.'

'Give it a rest Monty, I'm sick of you behaving like Chief Kommandant of the thermostat.'

'And I'm sick of you sneaking home and constantly switching the heating on during the day.'

'I just want to know what you are playing at – heating comes on, I switch it off, you switch it on as well you know.'

'SNEAKING? Monty – just get a life.'

Ralph listened from afar. Everything seemed to be going pretty much to plan. There was a similar set-to every night. The atmosphere was damaging to his feline sensibilities but he remained as tolerant as he could by keeping his eyes on the endgame. This was to come sooner than anticipated.

'Denise…we need to talk.'

'No Monty, we do nothing but talk. Since you started lording it over the house the trust has just gone.'

'You're telling me the trust has gone, that's a bit rich coming from you. I have finally put two and two together. You come home in the afternoons with your fancy man – put on the heating and think I won't notice.'

'Monty – get over yourself. There is no fancy man. I don't come home in the day any more – your smart technology has seen to that. Why would you trust me over what your Smartphone says? It may have saved a few pounds but at what cost? Just take your infernal technology somewhere else Monty – I've had enough.'

Ralph's whiskers twitched. He knew his work was done. There would be the inevitable toxic atmosphere during the staff redundancy exercise, but it would not be long before things were back to normal. Ralph revved up his purr in readiness for a return to the standard of high service he expected.

Sharing the Bacon

Nichola May

Gulls: much the same here, as anywhere.
Back home the gulls wedge side-by-side,
turn upside upon the tide
and follow fish shoals out of Uig Bay
as far as they can fly.
Here, gulls squat back-to-back,
Kerwark! at passers-by,
then hound the tourist clippers
up and down the Thames.

My kids, grown up,
remember nothing of back home.
Some weeks they find the time to come
and say what's good for me
—*cut down on fat*
—*get exercise*
—*a hobby would be good*
I tell them that I have a hobby now,
I like to sit and watch the birds.

They laugh, *in London, Dad*?
Aye, I know. Crazy.

People: much the same here, as anywhere.
Everyone except the gull is too preoccupied
with life to notice one old man,
a bacon sandwich in his hand.
We have a lot in common, gull and me,
most days, this bench here,
we take the time to share a slice of city life.
I eat the lean, he eats the fat,
we both can live guilt-free.

A Holiday Should Do the Trick!

Janet Bolam

'**D**addy, you promised we'd have a pool!' twelve year old Gabby howled. 'This is rubbish! All I can see are trees, trees, trees. And rocks'. She threw a stone off the terrace towards the banks of olive trees below.

'But look at the view' said her mother 'you can see the sea peeping through! It's really very pretty' 'What's the point of just seeing the sea?' Gabby stormed into the cottage bursting into loud sobs, brushing past her older sister who was grimly jabbing her i Phone.

'We can't even get a signal here. This place it total crap!'

'Language, Natalie!' rapped her father. Mark was at the end of his tether. It wasn't even his idea to come on this holiday, but Miranda insisted, something to do with reconnecting as a family. By the time they finished with this lot, Mark feared there would be plenty of reconnecting going on, but not in a good way.

'Time for dinner!' trilled Miranda as she set out tomatoes, cheese, bread and a dish of olive oil, then with a flourish lit some old candles she had found under the sink.

'Is this it?' Mark looked at the sparse table in dismay, his dreams of lamb souvlaki thwarted.

'Yup. All I could get' she returned brightly.

'Not very organised, are you?' volleyed Natalie and Gabby renewed her wailing. The ants, which until then had been invisible, made their way to the table attracted by the smell of the feast, followed swiftly by a chorus of mosquitoes. Mark could take this no longer.

'OK everyone, abandon ship and into the car. We're off to a taverna that has real food in it.'

It was late when they returned to the cottage and at first they noticed nothing, but when Miranda went to the bathroom, she was surprised to find the bathroom sink had fallen off the pedestal and was lying on the floor. The small window that was high up on the wall above the sink was open. Stunned, they finally realised they had been burgled.

'Albanians' concluded the policeman at the station the next day. 'It is always the Albanians. But we have it under control. Crime on this island is very unusual.'

The policeman laboriously recorded all the details in a ledger as the heat of the day mounted. Then he beckoned them to sit at a desk.

'Are you sure you want us to investigate this?' he started.

'Of course. We've been robbed!' exclaimed Mark.

'If you do decide to, you should know that it may take us up to a year.'

'Why would it take that long?'

The policeman shrugged his shoulders.

'You would have to wait for at least a year and then if we don't find anything, you would not be able to claim on your insurance. You understand me? And I'm afraid a robbery such as this is very low on our list of priorities. We are very busy and sadly, very understaffed…'

A silence broken by the whirr of the fan on the desk hung in the room.

'On the other hand,' the policeman continued, 'you could say you lost your possessions when you were out somewhere, say on a beach. You have insurance?' 'Why would we do that when we've been robbed?'

'If it is eventually proved to be a robbery, perhaps you get your things back. Perhaps not.'

Miranda eyed the girls who were leaning lethargically on the car bonnet sipping their cokes.

'In the car, now!' she barked as she slammed the door.

'So you just let them get away with not investigating a crime!' she snapped. 'You've agreed to lie to the insurance company and say we lost everything on a beach when we went for a swim? It's absurd! No wonder they say there's no crime here. Obviously there is! They're trying to hide it so no more tourists get robbed just like we have!'

'But this way we get another phone for Gabby and replace the i Pad. You're in cloud cuckoo land if you think we'd get anything back if we'd insisted on an investigation. Bad enough I've lost the dollars. Can't claim for them.'

'More fool you for bringing them!'

'So here we go,' chimed Natalie 'another glorious day on the best holiday we ever had!'

'And you can shut up!' shot Mark

'Don't you dare speak to her like that!' retorted Miranda 'it's not her fault that you've decided to perjure yourself to the insurance company!'

Natalie burst into tears 'I don't want to go back to the cottage. It's creepy. Someone must have been watching and waiting for us to go out last night! How do we know they won't be there again?'

'I hate this holiday and I hate you' moaned Gabby to no-one in particular.

In an attempt to find harmony, Miranda suggested they hire a boat.

'You can hire them for a day and sail right round the island. We could take a picnic and find a deserted beach?'

To her surprise this met with general approval and in an astonishingly short time, they were installed in their small boat and headed out of the harbour, laden with a huge bag of biscuits from the local bakery which they shared and called lunch. At first the coast was busy, but as they rounded the island, they found themselves alone, except for the large boats way out in the distance. Exposed on the harsher side of the island, the sea became choppy.

'I feel sick' moaned Gabby.

'I'm going to be sick. Can we land here?' rejoined Natalie.

They looked at the sheer cliff, and saw it was impossible to land. Natalie threw herself over to the side and was elaborately sick into the water. The boat rolled dangerously. Round the bay they came to a beach. It was no more than ten foot wide, backed by shrub-laden hills and, was deserted.

'Come and swim with me,' Gabby was pulling on her flippers and throwing small pebbles at Natalie, who was stretched out and covered in AmbreSolaire.

'No way, I don't want to get my hair wet.'

'You're so boring, Nat. All you want to do is get a tan so David Harewood will fancy you when you get home.' 'I do not! I hate David Harewood.'

'That's not what I heard. I heard you were…'

'Shut up! I hate you, you little creep!'

'Will you two stop bickering for once' said Miranda looking up from her Sarah Waters.

'Mum she won't come in the water with me!'

Mark, seeing Gabby dejected and forlorn with her flippers still attached, whisked her into his arms and ran for the sea.

'Daddy! You're funny!' Gabby giggled.

'Right!' he laughed 'who's for a snorkel?'

The lure of the crystal clear water was too much for Miranda and finally for an overheated Natalie. They were absorbed by a shoal of tiny silver fish that darted in and out of the rocks when a flick of triangular fin snaked its way between them. A shark in slow motion was heading towards Gabby who hadn't yet noticed it. A hundred thoughts bombarded Mark as he watched, helplessly as the fin made a graceful arch in the water and he croaked with relief 'A dolphin, a dolphin!'

The dolphin was heading to the shore, and as they paddled towards it, it slid almost completely out of the water and lay on the slope of the beach. As they approached it, they could see a series of cuts on its back.

'Look, it's been hurt' cried Gabby

'Caught under a boat propeller, I think' said Mark. 'The cuts don't look too deep. It's just winded and a bit shaken.' Natalie tentatively lowered her hand and stroked it. The dolphin was strange to touch, smooth, but with a grainy feel.

'It seems odd to call the dolphin it,' ventured Gabby 'I think she's a girl.'

'Perhaps we should keep her wet,' Miranda smiled as she filled an empty water bottle with sea water and poured it slowly over the dolphin's drying back. The four of them stroked her and kept a small stream of water running over her back for a good ten minutes, then decided they needed to help her back into the sea. Tucking towels under her grey bulk, they tried to pull her back into the water, tugging as gently as they could lest they hurt her, but once they managed to get her half submerged she rolled round and slithered down into the water. With a cheer, Natalie and Gabby followed.

'She's gone!' sighed Gabby.

'No she hasn't' cried Natalie as the dolphin re-emerged a few feet from her, 'I think she wants to play.'

The dolphin stayed around the family, diving and surfacing and swimming around them, weaving between their legs, making sudden jumps out of the water, and occasionally butting them with her long nose. She even joined in when they threw the beach ball to each other in the water when to their wonder and delight, she nosed it along the surface.

'She's just like a puppy!' exclaimed Natalie

Homeward bound, the car grumbled along the dusty tarmac and then began to hobble and finally ground to a halt. They were high in the hills far from the main tourist trail, and not another car or person to be seen. They pushed it to the side of the road and called the hire company.

'They're coming to get us as soon as they can,' said Mark, resigned because he knew how long things took on Paxos. They walked across the scrubland to find a smooth rock to sit on. The soothing undertone of bees and cicadas was interrupted by the tapping bells of a herd of goats and the gentle wind blew scents of oregano and orange blossom. They made themselves comfortable, leaning on each other, dozing.

Gabby, deciding to explore, picked her way through the prickly shrubs towards a small rocky outcrop.

'Wow!' she cried, 'this is the top of a cliff!'

The others wandered over to join her.

'Do you know what?' said Mark, 'if I'm not mistaken, we can see the dolphin beach from here.' They followed his pointing finger and all agreed that the small line of sand they could see round the bay from the caves was 'their dolphin' beach.

'Shall we go back there tomorrow, just in case she comes back?' Natalie's eyes shone with excitement and they began to plan the day.

'I've got fresh bread, water and tomatoes in the car,' Miranda remembered.

'Perfect' said Natalie

Once Bitten …

Kathleen Daly

What do you do about a dog that's continuously being passed over? You can't see why. He's a perfectly nice little terrier, bright-eyed, wagging tail, no side to him … yet the visitors don't take him home. It may be the dog that doesn't find the people he wants, and not the other way round.

Benson stretched. All dogs do that, but not the way Benson did. Benson had spent months watching his previous owner's yoga DVDs. He was aware of every sinew, muscle, ligament, in his legs, felt the power ripple along his back and under his belly, and let his mind float up and away from the rescue centre. Not that he had any complaints about his current berth. He got meals on time, and plenty of attention from the humans here. He yawned and rolled on his back, sporting a pink belly dappled with black and white spots. What was there not to like? Well, a bit more scope for ratting and rabbiting would have been welcome, and quieter neighbours.

Thud, thud, thud. At it again. A total obsessive. Benson opened one eye and followed the trajectory of the tennis ball. Wall, floor, bounce, grab. The gyrating red and white fur made him queasy. A border collie, what else? They were all loopy; it came from trying to stay awake when you were counting all those sheep.

He opened the other eye. There was a tasty black and red spaniel on that side. He'd have liked a closer acquaintance with her. They'd snuffled under the wire, but that was as far as they'd got. She was desperate to get back her previous humans. Benson tried to calm her down. You had to take life as it came.

The year before, he'd been with devoted humans with a young kid who liked nothing better than throwing balls for Benson. One day they just hadn't come home. Of course he'd pined in the centre. But, hey, you toughen up. And you get very choosy. You don't want to be let down again. So Benson had scowled for his photo. He was no lap dog.

One or two visitors had asked to see him regardless. They just didn't match up to his standards. The first pair wanted a dog to help them get fit. He'd heard that before. They'd soon go back to being couch potatoes, and what would happen to his walks? The second lot wanted a dog to keep their overactive kid occupied. Oh my, no chance. Benson intended to keep his ears, eyes and other appendages, and didn't want to have to snap to make that clear. He'd focused and sent out those vibes that put humans off without them quite knowing why. The humans at the centre had been very sorry, made a special

fuss of him and slipped him extra treats and toys …
enough to make a dog laugh.

Benson knew his own powers. So he just waited 'til
those extra special people came along as he knew they
would, one day soon.

The main gate clanged. The alpha female, the one in
charge of the others, came into his run. She chattered on
as humans do. He didn't pay much attention, just did the
usual waggy tail and vacant grin that kept humans happy,
until she produced his lead and said the magic word, the
one that sounded like a pup yipping. *Agility.* That meant
he'd go out into the green field steaming with wild
smells, and when he'd had his fill of those, over the
hurdles, through tunnels and the up and down thing
humans called 'see-saw'. The other humans always got
excited when he did that, clapped their hands together.
Benson liked to beat his own score, covering the distance
in even fewer heartbeats than the previous time, feeling
his lungs burn and his paws pound.

Today something had changed. A youngish female
human was leaning over the gate, watching him. She had
a thin face, pointed nose, a mass of dark hair hanging
onto her shoulders and lively eyes. The eyes were very
important.

She knelt down and stretched out her hand. Benson
sniffed. Something meaty. He leant back on his haunches
and put his paws against his chest. Damn foolish really,
but it produced the goods. He took the treat delicately.
First impressions were very important. As he'd told that
collie, no more treats if you take their fingers off. He
crunched on the chunk of meat and biscuit, and licked

her fingers. She didn't draw back her hand. That was a good sign. She and the other human made those lazy sounds, much harder to understand than a yelp or a bark. He kept hearing the word 'Sue'. That was probably her name then. She called to him, and they were off.

She knew what she was doing. She hardly seemed to move, but she was always in the right place, pointing out the next bit of equipment. Benson had never gone round that course so fast. He leapt and barked and she caught him in her arms and hugged him.

Then he saw the male. Tall and thin, and covered in black. He had that pale skin that humans got when they hardly ever set foot outside and he had those black disks over his eyes. Benson hated it when people covered up their eyes, and he couldn't work out what they were up to. He inhaled, exhaled. He'd have a hard job not nipping the louse if he came too close. He mustn't put 'Sue' off. But the male totally ignored him, putting a hand on her shoulder as if he owned her.

This was bad. What did 'Sue' think of the male? Were they really bonded? What if the male lived with Sue? Benson thought not. Sue was quivering. They didn't know each other well then. Humans that had been together a long time generally didn't react much.

Ah, she'd knelt down to him again, was stroking his back and tummy. Benson wriggled and made mock growling noises, rolled belly up. She clipped on his lead, and he trotted along beside her. The male drifted after them, crinkling his face as humans do when they're fed up. Benson could have told him that nothing in life was perfect. Still, any intelligent dog knew how to split up an unfortunate pairing. Benson could cope. Just give him till the next full moon.

Rich Man, Poor Man ...

Jackie Vickers

Jerome had been advised to take up the offer of a temporary job. Working for a charity looks good on a CV and, while it is not always easy dealing with the homeless, being an outreach worker in this town would not be particularly onerous. He was allocated to the north-eastern section, which was bounded by the ring-road, the river and the high street. All the homeless in this area were to be approached, befriended and persuaded into *Blair House*, the homeless shelter facing St Chad's parish church.

He met Henry during his first week. Things got off to a bad start when Henry claimed to be hungry, yet refused Jerome's discarded sandwich. It had a bite taken out of it, which, in Henry's view, made it unacceptable.

'It's perfectly good food,' argued Jerome. 'I bought it at that expensive deli in the market place. I just didn't fancy the chutney.'

Henry tore off the chewed end and gave the rest to his dog.

Jerome could see that getting Henry into the shelter might be a challenge. The next day he stuffed an old sweater into his bag and went to look for him. Henry looked at the sweater, turning it over and over and finally laying it out on the pavement. He gave it a nudge with his boot.

'It's got a hole in it.'

Jerome had at one time, been attached to this sweater. 'It's pure new wool,' he said with pride. 'And anyway, there's a hole in the one you're wearing.'

'This is my hole. I don't want to be wearing someone else's hole. What else have you got in there then?' He peered into Jerome's bag.

'New trainers - unwanted present.'

'Why don't you want them?'

'I've got two pairs the same already,' Jerome started to pull up the zip. 'I'm going to swap them.'

'I can save you the trouble,' grinned Henry, showing a couple of gaps in his teeth.

It was proving very difficult to get Henry interested in any sort of work. He was obviously set on remaining homeless and came out with the same old excuse.

'They wants an address.'

But Jerome wasn't sure Henry would be employable, as he wouldn't be parted from that scruffy hound for a start.

'Anyway, I got a job.' He was sitting on the steps of the war-memorial, surrounded by his plastic bags. 'I performs a public service.' He wrapped his arms around his chest and snorted. 'Folk gives me their loose change. It makes them feel good.'

'I expect they feel sorry for you.'

'Soon wears off, though and they're off spending again. That's the trouble with this job, you can't influence public morality.' Henry shivered. 'So, what brings you to charity work then?'

'It's a job where you can make a difference.' It was an argument that Jerome's friends and family often used, but he wasn't sure Henry understood. 'Cleaning up the streets by getting homeless people into shelters seems like something worth working for.'

Henry thought about it. 'What happens when you've herded us all into a shelter, eh? Will you be out of a job then?'

'That won't happen, people like you are awkward and won't go.'

'That's because hostels won't take Charley here.' Henry nodded towards his dog who was tied to the lamp-post with a piece of string. He stamped his feet and blew on his fingers.

'Why don't you get rid of the dog and spend the night somewhere warm?'

Henry appeared to give this some thought. He bent down and scratched behind Charley's ears. 'Do you have a brother?'

'I do, as a matter of fact,' said Jerome.

'Well, say you was both on the street and the hostel would only take one of you.' He raised his eyebrows, then gathered up his plastic bags. Looking over his shoulder he said, 'I thought you'd been to university? They didn't learn you much.' With a grin that looked more like a leer, he untied his dog and set off. 'See ya!'

'Say you won the lottery,' Henry said. It was a few days later and they were both rocking to and fro on the swings in the park. 'How much money would you give me?'

'Not much! You'd only drink it.'

'Selfish bastard!' he laughed and untied his dog. 'See ya!' Henry ran off with Charley. He could move at quite a speed, now he was wearing Jerome's trainers.

A few minutes later he came jogging back. 'You never asked me what *I'd* do with the winnings,' Henry said.

'Well, what would you do with the winnings?'

'I'd build a proper hostel for starters.' Henry smirked.

'*Blair House* **is** a proper hostel and you'd know that if you ever bothered to come and have a look round.'

'A proper one takes dogs,' he snapped.

Jerome sighed. 'If you had won that much money you wouldn't *need* to live in a hostel.'

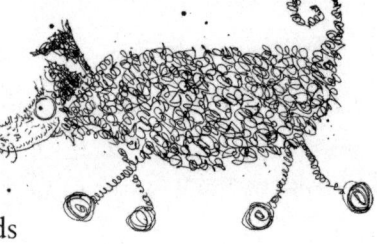

'All my homeless friends

have dogs! What about them, eh?' Henry knelt down and buried his face in his dog's unkempt coat.

Later that week Henry ran out of an off-licence with a couple of bottles and, seeing Jerome, called out, 'Come and celebrate!' and set off in the direction of the park. Jerome, who felt rather cold, despite his new ski-ing jacket, was reluctant.

'We'll soon warm up with some of this.' Henry waved his bottles. 'I've always wanted to see what the good stuff was like.' He was weaving in and out of the crowds at speed. The park was deserted and he made for the swings.

'So, what are we celebrating?' Jerome squinted up at the weak winter sun and rubbed his hands together.

'Have a swig of this and I'll tell you. Remember we was talking about the lottery? Charley here was nosing by the bins and found a ticket. I've checked the number.' He leaned down to pat his hound. 'It was the one they said no-one claimed last month. Hostels for dogs - eh Charley? And good booze with steak every night.'

Jerome stared at him. That ticket could have been the passport to weeks on some beach in California or Mexico. While Henry burbled on about his plans, Jerome considered their relationship and wondered how much money Henry could be induced to part with. After all, he'd been pretty decent to him recently, with the trainers and so on. Henry started on the second bottle but soon his speech became slurred from drinking so much on an empty stomach. He stumbled off the swing, stretched out on the ground with his hound nuzzling up to him, and was soon asleep.

It was a moment's job to rescue the ticket and Jerome went home to pack.

Around midnight, four scruffy-looking heavies started thumping on his door. When he surfaced in the morning the ticket had gone.

Blair House had been renamed *Henry's Hotel*. Jerome didn't recognise Henry at first. He was clean-shaven and wore a suit.

'Charley looks well,' Jerome said. The dog looked up at him and growled.

Henry explained that Charley had been the first to try the new on-site grooming facilities for dogs. He was sorry there were no rooms available, but suggested to Jerome that sleeping rough might be character-building.

'It's full of dog-owners, see, now we've fitted the place up with these canine shelters.'

The new outreach worker was not sympathetic, even when Jerome explained how he used to believe in goodness, the milk of human kindness, and that sort of thing. It was difficult, now, to believe in anything, sitting out in the cold. It was too cold to think, even.

'But I'll be finding work soon,' Jerome assured him, 'just as soon as I have an address. And while I'm waiting I might get a dog.'

Having a Ball

Kathleen Daly

'My dancing days are over. I only ever did it to land women. Once I met you, I was glad to give it up.'

Cindy wrinkled her nose. Prince Charming, eh? When she'd first met her husband, he'd carried hardly any spare flesh and had sported a full head of golden curls. Now his middle had spread and his hair had receded, she wondered what she'd seen in him. Royalty?Money, maybe? She pushed the crumbs of croissant round her plate. Did all fairy-tale romances end in such banality?

He looked up from his Blackberry.

'My dear, these popular TV programmes aren't for us. Look what "It's a Knock Out" did to the Windsors. Took them three decades to recover.' He peered over the rim of his glasses. 'Now that's a thought. Dogs! Why don't you get a couple of pedigree corgis? That's what people like us do when we're past the first flush.'

She started to say, 'Not me, not where I came from!' but he'd already retreated into his virtual world. She thrust back her chair, which hit the marble with a crash. No reaction, so she flounced out of the room.

'When the going gets tough, the tough go shopping!' she resolved. And to remind herself of her harsh upbringing, she ignored the Merc.and took the Underground. Somehow she didn't have her usual enthusiasm for Stella McCartney, Chanel, or even Reiss.

'I'm so bored,' she thought, 'I'll hop out at random, just so long as it's somewhere I haven't been before.'

She shut her eyes and counted ten stations. Then she got off. The streets were unfamiliar. She never knew quite what made her push open that particular door. Maybe it was having to climb that ladder to the top herself, that made her want to help others down on their luck. She'd only meant to donate something. Then she saw him. It wasn't just hot flushes, she hadn't felt like that since THE Ball. Maybe it was that fine aristocratic nose, or the keen brown eyes, that air of alertness, of someone who wasn't going to give in. Whatever he'd done to end up in here, he must get a second chance.

As she always looked after the home front, her husband didn't ask any questions when he saw the new boy.

'This is Buttons,' she said. 'He's my new bodyguard.'

'That's good,' said her husband. 'I don't like you wandering about on your own.'

She had to admit Buttons scrubbed up well. There was that something about him that made her think of glamour, and tuxedos. Then she had the idea. It took a bit of research, and a lot of commitment. It was far more competitive than she'd realised. They took lessons together, twice, three times a week. Every weekend they took off together. She hired different taxi firms, so no one would give the game away to her husband. She couldn't bear him to suspect and feel jealous, or worse, make fun of them.

Buttons was so elegant. He fixed his eyes on hers and gazed into her soul. He seemed to know what she was thinking before she knew it herself. They started to make a name for themselves on the circuit. Poky little halls with hardly room to move. Well-appointed church rooms, with carpeted floors. Old cinemas converted to bingo, then to dance halls. Hippodromes! They danced through the too-small-to-mention, the local, county, district, regional qualifiers; the quarters, the semis; the national finals. Then the international!

'What shall I wear?' she said. 'I must have a special dress!' But he just gave her that gaze that melted her, as if to say, whatever you wear, I adore you! She'd always liked the quiet sort.

'It will be a surprise, then,' she cooed. She shooed him out, and texted her favourite designer in Paris.

'Something *typique* of your country, I think, Madame," he said.

She frowned. 'We're a tax haven. We launder money. We can't do much else. Ruritania's all mountains and trees, you see. Oh, there's a bit of tourism. And cheese, I suppose.'

He sniffed. 'Let us pursue the money angle, then. *L'argent*. Yes, I see it now!'

The dress arrived. Her heart pounded as she took the gold lamé lid off the box. The fine material cascaded through her hands. The bodice, in silver, dropped to a low waist, almost twenties style. The skirt was knee-length, layered thin silk gauze embroidered with leaves in silver and black. Only as she fingered the leaves did she realise they were made from dollars, pounds, and euros. She called Buttons in to see it. He gazed open-mouthed.

'That solves the music problem, darling.' She kissed his nose. 'It has to be "Hey Big Spender"!'

By this time they were running together every morning to keep fit. And that's when the unthinkable happened. The snow was melting into slushy mud, and Buttons skidded. When he got up, he was limping.

'Oh, my dearest? Not a ligament strain! We must get that seen to at once!'

The specialist looked stern.

'Rest,' he said. 'Then physiotherapy. Then hydrotherapy.'

'We have a pool in the palace," she panted.

Practice was out of the question. Even if Buttons recovered in time, they'd have to change the routine. The high lifts, standing on shoulders and back flips were out of the question. She walked through the new steps and manoeuvres by herself. He watched, memorising, nursing his bandaged limb. She couldn't believe it when they got the 'all clear', only a week before their Big Day.

'Shall we scratch, my dearest?' she said. 'Do we dare go through with it, with hardly any time to prepare?' For answer, he nuzzled her neck.

On the night, the blazing lights and yells of the crowd made her want to faint. But he was unperturbed. The moment they stepped on the floor and the first beats of the music rang out across the arena, the noise hushed. The spotlights set her dress off against the stark black and white of her partner. She forgot her nerves. They danced as they'd never danced before. He plucked leaves off her dress one by one and tossed them into the air like confetti, till she was left only in the glimmering silk. The crowd roared. Twirls and whirls, sashaying round each other, reversing through legs, even the odd leap and lift, in spite of that leg.

At the end, the crowd went wild. Cindy's eyes smarted as she hugged her partner.

'I can never thank you enough, Buttons!" she said. "My dream's come true at last. It may not be 'Strictly Come Dancing', but how many people win Freestyle to Music at Crufts?" And she kissed his black and white fur, before throwing him his ball.

Buckland and the Antediluvian Hyenas' Den

Ann Edwards

Oxford 1823

The Reverend William Buckland was not a vain man. In fact in some quarters he was considered careless of his appearance. If he had a vanity it was for his magnificent eyebrows. They were brilliant white and framed his brow with an extravagant curl extending two inches from his forehead. The furthest tips of them were tinted a pale yellow from the nicotine from his pipe. Buckland used them as a means of communication, similar to a rock hopper penguin - waggled they expressed pleasure; lowered displeasure.

He was sitting in his study sipping a cup of tea and nibbling at toast while Mrs Buckland stood behind him, combing out the eyebrow dandruff. As she combed, snowflakes of dandruff drifted and settled onto the ginger fur of the large cat sleeping on Buckland's knee. The cat would be devastated when it noticed and it would take over an hour of thorough washing to restore his coat to its customary high standard.

Buckland had been recently studying his pigeons and had come to the conclusion that mutual grooming strengthens the pair bond. Mrs Buckland held the view that there was not much mutual about this eyebrow grooming activity but for the reasons of marital harmony kept her views to herself. Buckland took her silence to mean 'pair bond reinforced'. He was happily writing in his head a treatise entitled *'Observations of the effects of mutual grooming and the calming effect on the wives of clergymen'*, when their harmony was interrupted by a knock at the door. The maid stuck her head in and said in a resigned voice:

'There's a man at the door with a hyena.'

'Splendid,' shouted Buckland leaping from his chair.

December 1822

Yorkshire is a long way away. Buckland was on his way to Kirkland Cave in Yorkshire. He had received a letter from a Mr Billy Braithwaite informing him that the said gentleman had found some bones in a cave. Mr Braithwaite had heard that Mr Buckland was a collector of natural history and that for the small remuneration of five guineas he would take Buckland to them. Buckland replied by return that he was on his way.

In Buckland's absence Christ Church and Oxford breathed a sigh of relief and settled down to enjoy the peace and quiet.

The journey was to take two weeks, not the two days advised by the Royal Turnpike Association handbook and gazetteer in itsroute-finder section. The delay was because Buckland could not pass an open rock face without leaping down to examine every fallen pebble. Bess, his black mare, had grown so accustomed to this behaviour that she now regularly stopped of her own volition whether Buckland now wanted her to or not.

They were met in Kirkland by Mr Billy Braithwaite and his dog. Man and dog led Buckland over the slippery clints and grikes towards the entrance of the cave eighty feet up the cliff face.

'Ready?' Braithwaite enquired.

Buckland tucked his trousers into his socks and said 'Ready.' They entered the mouth of the cave. It was pitch dark, lit only by the trembling light from Braithwaite's lantern. His dog followed, its natural exuberance curbed by the gloom of the place. The roof of the cave lowered and as they progressed they were forced down onto hands and knees. They squeezed through a fissure in the limestone to emerge into a cavern. It was silent, apart from the rhythmic drip of water from stalactite to stalagmite. Mud sucked at their boots as they walked.

Billy Braithwaite placed the lantern on the ground. The candle flickered in the draught but illuminated the floor of the cave. They were standing on hundreds of bones, bones of all shapes and sizes. Skulls, clavicles, scapulars, tarsals, metatarsals, hooves, femurs, horns, fragments, shards, splinters and thousands of teeth. To Buckland's joy he thought he could see the remnants of a tusk. His mind raced. What was he looking at?

The first bone Buckland picked up was the jaw bone of an ass. Next, he found the shoulder blade of a mastodon, then a deer antler, the foot of a tapir and then joy of joys, small round pebble like nuggets with tiny bones and splinters visible within them.

'Look, look, perfectly preserved *album graecum*' he called excitedly.

'Looks like a turd to me,' replied Braithwaite.

'You are a very perceptive man. That, I believe is the layman's term for them. Or shit, crap, pooh, plop plops, in Yiddish it's *bubkes*. But no matter, these are not fresh faeces they are, in my view, very old turds indeed. See...' said Buckland as he picked one of the objects up, sniffed it and then licked it, 'No smell or taste' Braithwaite looked pale.

The dog was having a good time as well. It had never seen so many bones. It picked one up and gave it an exploratory gnaw but gave up after a few minutes, disappointed at the absence of marrow.

'A hyena skull definitely a hyena skull,' said Buckland, handing the specimen to Braithwaite to put in his sack. He picked up the bone the dog had been chewing.

'Look at the teeth marks on this. They look so fresh. Gnu leg bone, obviously a gnu, any idiot could tell this was a gnu, look at the gnuness of it. It's been worried by something with incredibly powerful jaws. Teeth marks made by a pack of hyenas do you think?'

Braithwaite shrugged and kicked the dog out of the way. They worked collecting bones for hours. When the sack was so heavy Braithwaite could barely lift it, they stopped. It was raining as they emerged from the cave, penetrating the Yorkshire rain.

'On the same day all the fountains of the great deep were broken up, and the windows of heaven were opened, and the rain was upon the earth forty days and forty nights,' intoned Buckland as they trudged back down the moor.

'Aye thae's in Yorkshire now, lad' responded Braithwaite.

For a moment the sun broke through the clouds, illuminating the drizzle. Buckland gasped as a rainbow arched in front of them.

'It's a sign' shouted Buckland to the retreating backs of Braithwaite and the dog.

'Daft sod,' thought Braithwaite.

August 1823

In his study in Corpus Christi College, Buckland sat and thought. The specimens he had collected revealed themselves, after much study, to be bones of hippopotamus, elephant, rhinoceros, bison, tiger, gnu, elk, wolf, rat, bird, mouse and hyena, lots of hyenas. These bones were now pinned for reference on the walls of his study, giving it the look of a Zoroastrian ossuary. A look Buckland had always admired. His large brain ran round and round the problem, worrying at, it herding it into shape, only for it to make a run for it and the solution to scatter. He wrote:

Hypothesis. Then continued, Hyena skull, hyena teeth, Gnu bones (and assorted others, some animals extinct, none native to England) with teeth marks. Were the animals eaten by hyenas? How had they got there? How old are they?

He imagined three thousand years ago the fetid darkness of the cave. A pack of savage hyenas fighting over the carcass of the elephant they had dragged back to their lair. There would have been snarling and gnashing of teeth not dissimilar to the dining room in Christ Church on roast dinner night. He doodled for a bit, drank some tepid tea, chewed a crust of toast left over from elevenses and stroked the cat. After some time he realised that what he was staring at was Wombwell and Bostock's Beast show setting up camp in Christ Church meadow. The Beast show arrived every year in time for the St Giles Fair. The sound of lions roaring, camels braying and elephants trumpeting echoed across the lawns. The smell of the animals drifted into Buckland's study and the cat looked subdued. Mrs.Buckland came in with some fresh tea.

'Do you think hyenas could drag an elephant into a cave?' she asked helpfully.

He ignored her.

She pressed on 'Do hyenas eat hippopotamus?

He pretended he hadn't heard her. How was a man to concentrate with a woman babbling on like that? He did some more thinking, fed the tortoise, smoked a pipe, calmed his mind by re arranging his fly collection*, and then he GOT IT.

What he needed was a live hyena. He could then compare the marks made by the teeth of the living hyena with the teeth marks on the bones from the cave. If they matched, and he was confident they would, he had found, as he suspected, an antediluvian hyenas'den. But he didn't have a hyena. His eye was drawn again out of the window to the distant bustle of the Beast Show.

Mr Bostock could barely believe his luck when he read the note from Buckland. Yes he did have a hyena. It was ancient, decrepit, it smelt, it had rotten teeth, it was moth eaten, incontinent. Nor were these the only problems with the beast - it cringed when any one approached, it was a surprisingly fussy eater and in protest at the quality of food Mr.Bostock supplied, it had eaten its own front leg, so now it hopped. It was now so repellent that no one was prepared to pay the sixpence he charged to look at it and the thing was a bloody nuisance. He'd be glad to see the back of it. He had a plan to replace the hyena with a more commercial coypu and advertise it as: 'The biggest rat in the world.' Now who wouldn't pay to see that?

As he now stood at the door of Buckland's study with the three legged animal at his side it urinated on the mat. Far from putting him off when Buckland first saw the hyena it was love at first sight.

'I'll take it,' he told Mr Bostock, grasping the piece of string that served as its lead. 'A spotted cape hyena. Is it male or female?' he asked.

Bostock blushed, 'It's hard to tell, Sir.'

Buckland waggled his eyebrows in astonishment. 'You mean you don't know? Didn't your mother teach you about the birds and the bees?'

'I mean you can't tell, Sir. You can't tell girl hyenas from boy hyenas, because they both have ...' and here Mr Bostock looked exceedingly embarrassed at having to use this word in front on a man of the cloth: 'Pinkles'.

'Pinkles?' asked Buckland.

'Podgers,' Bostock tried again.

'Sorry, I'm not with you?'

'Bostock, shifting from foot to foot, mumbled 'Pizzles.'

Buckland looked ecstatic. 'Are you telling me she has a pseudo- penis?'

Bostock scratched his head and said 'I think so.'

And so Hermi, short for Hermaphrodite, which is what Buckland called her, came to live in the kennels of Corpus Christi College. Buckland fed her on the finest cow bones the college butcher, Mr Grimshaw, could supply. Buckland took her for walks, well more accurately hops, around Oxford and she became something of a celebrity. Buckland made a forensic study of the teeth marks found on Hermi's leftovers. He compared these with the marks found on the bones from the cave. He concluded that the origin of the marks on both sets of bones were indeed from hyenas, as he had first thought. He compared Hermaphrodite's fresh faeces with the *album graeca* from the cave and concluded they too were from the same source. How had this den of hyenas with all its extinct animals come to be in Yorkshire?

Buckland decided that the only plausible explanation, given the evidence, was that the cave, the hyenas and the remains of their prey, all animals of darkest Africa, not native to England, had been drowned in the deluge sent by God to destroy the earth, Book of Genesis Chapter Six :

'When Noah was six hundred years old, God, saddened at the wickedness of mankind, decided to send a great deluge to destroy all life. And so the Flood came, and all life was extinguished, except for those who were with Noah'

(As a young theology student, Buckland had calculated that Noah must have had on board 45,000 animals. This must have created logistical problems that only the hand of God could have solved).

Buckland had hanging on his study walls the actual remains of the animals that didn't walk in two by two. This was going to be one of the most exciting scientific discoveries of the century. It would nip in the bud the ridiculous talk of us all being descended from monkeys, coming from that annoying lot in Cambridge –Rev. Henslow and his latest protégé some youth called Darwin.

Unknown to Buckland, poor rotten-toothed Hermaphrodite could only suck the juices out of the bones she was given. When no one was watching, (scientific observation of the living was not one of

Buckland's strong suits) a pack of foxhounds in the next door kennel organised bone raids, rioting into Hermaphrodite's cage to have an intense grapple with her bony supper before being beaten back into their own quarters by the whippers-in.

★ Buckland collected flies. He had started as a boy at Blundells School in Devon. He now had boxes and boxes of flies. All neatly skewered to pieces of card with the specimen names, date of capture and location. He estimated there could be five thousand different species of fly in England. He was up to three thousand two hundred and six specimens, so still lots to do.

Also published in Imagine Oxford edited by Jackie Vickers

Weighing it All Up

Wendy Greenberg

S low autumn light stumbled through the curtains
across Stella's wrinkled features – signalling decision
time. Should she stay or should she go? Through the
tenebrous hours she had been weighing up her options.
She turned into the magnet of Eddie's warmth observing
his breath rising and falling, sleep enveloping every
familiar feature whilst she lay shrouded in her regular
insomnia. She laid her hand across his back and sunk into
the precious marshmallow moments beside him before
she began today's leap of faith.

She had met Charles at work. He had come with his
team to present to the board. By the time they won the
contract, Charles had insinuated himself into Stella's life.
She had not been looking for love but after that first
heady evening together she had not been hard to reel in.
They fell into an easy habit with one another and the year
had begun to slip away when he startled her.

'When I'm with you Stella, my life feels complete, stay with me, come and live with me'

He had reached for her, gently covering her hand and brushing it with his lips

'I love you' and as he pulled her close and held her tightly she whispered, realising, that it was true:

'And I love you too Charles.'

She pulsed with desire for this striking man with the velvet voice. His words vibrated through her. But all along there had been Eddie. Handsome, loyal, gorgeous Eddie, who always stood by her. How could she choose?

Charles knew about Eddie and despite the living arrangements did not consider him a serious rival but Eddie can only have guessed about Charles from Stella's long absences. When Stella was home he silently inveigled himself into her affection with ease. He wriggled into Stella's arms and she stroked his head, embracing him as if nothing could possibly change their close bond.

Stella pulled back the bedclothes preparing to rise and Eddie stirred. She swallowed and sighed. The maelstrom in the pit of her stomach raged as she picked up the phone beside the bed. Eddie was suddenly very awake, his sage coloured eyes expectant. She replaced the receiver.

'Eddie…I have to talk to you'

They looked at each other for a moment and Stella's heart melted. She couldn't leave Eddie, what had she been thinking? She would have to break it off with

Charles. She got out of bed and, with the relief of having made a decision, smiled at Eddie. He wrapped himself around her legs purring as his tail caressed her. He had no regrets, if sensitivity to cats was a deal breaker for Charles, so be it - after all faint heart never won fair lady!

Also published in Imagine Oxford edited by Jackie Vickers

Out of Africa

Andrew Bax

The final stage of her journey was a triumph. On the morning of 9 July 1827, escorted by the royal cavalry and crowds of fascinated onlookers, she walked the final nine miles from le Jardin du Roi to be presented to King Charles X. He was enchanted by her and soon all Paris adored her too. She became the subject of affectionate songs and satire, and inspired new fashions, clothes and home furnishings. She came to be called Zarafa – literally 'charming' or 'lovely one' in Arabic, and for a generation of French men and women who had suffered the deprivations of revolution, Napoleonic wars and the humiliation of defeat, she was unbelievably exotic. They were fascinated by the length of Zarafa's legs and neck, and mesmerised by her large, beautiful eyes, shaded by a fringe of curving lashes. Before her arrival, there were few who knew that such a creature existed but, by the end of August, over one hundred thousand people had been to see her. Zarafa was a giraffe.

She had been brought to Paris at immense cost as a gift from Muhammad Ali, an illiterate Albanian rogue whose ambition and tyranny eventually led him to become the Ottoman Viceroy of Egypt. Once in power, he built up a huge army of Sudanese slaves, trained by French mercenaries, which he used to invade his neighbours and increase his influence with his overlord, the Sultan of Turkey. He then set about ingratiating himself with France in order to obtain her support for his next planned expansion – the conquest of Greece, and Zarafa was to become his pawn in this game of international diplomacy. It was a sordid negotiation of greed, duplicity and, in the end, failure, but Zarafa's serene dignity rose above it all.

The plot was hatched in 1824 and orders were sent to the Viceroy's slaving garrison in Khartoum for the capture of a baby giraffe. Arab hunters were despatched two hundred miles further south into the Ethiopian savannah, which was teeming with wildlife. In the fine balance between predator and prey, healthy, adult giraffes were among the few animals whose only enemy was man. And man had hunted them for millennia: their thick and beautifully-marked hide was valued for making shields, sandals and drums; their tendons and bones for making musical instruments; and their meat was said to be delicious. Giraffes can outrun a horse over short distances and their kick can be lethal, but horsemen had perfected a method of chasing them in relays until they tired and were close enough to be hamstrung.

Zarafa, a female calf, was just two months old and only five feet tall when hunters finally brought down her mother. It would have been a bloody business but part of the natural order for survival in those regions. An older, weaned calf would have panicked and died either by resisting capture or in self-imposed starvation. However, Zarafa's hunters calmed her, fed her with milk and succeeded in transferring the maternal bond to themselves. She was strapped by her hooves to a camel and the meat from her mother was divided among four more. This sad little caravan then began its journey north.

At Khartoum Zarafa beguiled the hardened soldiers and their dispirited, newly-caught slaves, who treated her as a pet. During the next sixteen months she became completely accustomed to human company and her growing strength would enable her to endure the long journey that lay ahead. That began in a felucca, the sailing craft of the region, together with a cargo of female slaves bound for Cairo; at each of the six sets of cataracts below Khartoum all of them had to be off-loaded while the felucca was dragged over. Eventually they reached the calmer waters of the Nile and sailed downstream to the Mediterranean port of Alexandria, a total distance of over two thousand miles. There Zarafa spent the next three months recuperating in the palace grounds of the viceroy himself, where she first became acquainted with Atir, a former slave from the Sudan, who was to become her constant companion for the rest of her life.

In the meantime, arrangements were being made for her transport to Marseilles - at a cost of four thousand five hundred Francs, an enormous sum at the time. Still unweaned, she lived entirely on milk, up to twenty-five gallons a day. Her entourage was joined by three African, hump-backed cows to keep her well-supplied. All were loaded onto a Sicilian brigantine with a hole cut in the deck so that Zarafa could stand upright. By now, so much had been invested in Zarafa, both financially and politically, that her welfare became of paramount importance. The hole through the deck was carefully padded to make sure that her neck was not bruised by the movement of the ship, and a canopy protected her head against sun and rain. Already she had become 'le bel Animal du Roi' and heads would roll if she came to any harm.

The voyage to Marseilles took thirty-two days. The first that Atir and Zarafa would have seen of Europe would be the volcanic plume of Mount Etna, visible from below the horizon. Like many ships travelling between Europe, Africa and Asia, they anchored to rest the crew and replenish stores off Messina, in the narrow channel between Sicily and the toe of Italy. The ever-present threat of plague quarantined them on board but they would have been exposed to unfamiliar sights, sounds and tastes as they became surrounded by small boats offering them wine, water, fruit and vegetables, for which payment was made in coin dropped into pots of vinegar to prevent infection.

News that a 'cameleopard' – the head and neck of a camel, the spots of a leopard, was on board one of the ships outside Messina soon spread. Zarafa was not the first giraffe to be seen in Italy; some three hundred and fifty years earlier, the Sultan of Egypt sent a young female to the Medicis in Florence, like Zarafa, in the hope of gaining political favour. Contemporary accounts describe how, every day, she was taken to the noble houses of the city, 'to take food from the hands of the ladies of

Florence,' who enjoyed the novelty of feeding her through their upper-storey windows. And from the beginning of the Roman Empire, giraffes were among the thousands of exotic animals that were slaughtered and made to fight for the entertainment of the masses. To survive the journey to Rome the giraffes would have been caught young enough to tame, and reared purely for their spectacular death.

History does not record how Zarafa took to ocean travel. It would have been an experience entirely alien to an animal whose natural habitat was among acacia tress in tropical grassland. Her long legs and neck gave her a centre of gravity quite unsuited to the pitch and roll of a sailing ship and Zarafa, and her cows, probably suffered terribly from seasickness.

Outside a small scientific circle, the existence of giraffes was unknown in France, but the authorities in Marseilles had been alerted to the imminent arrival of an unusual animal on its way to the king. Whereas few details exist about the first part of Zarafa's journey, French bureaucracy provides us with an exhaustive documentary archive of how it continued. There still exist, for example, the invoices for renting the boat which transferred Zarafa and the cows to their quarantine facility outside the city, and the cost of needle, thread, measuring tape and cloth with which to make her a blanket. The prefect of Marseilles took his responsibilities so seriously that he ordered the immediate construction of a stable in the gardens of his mansion – one with a particularly high roof and, because winter was approaching, to be insulated with 'straw matting'. Costs were growing and so was Zarafa; while she was there she grew to eleven feet, six inches. The prefect reported, 'She loves very much to leave her stable and, when she is walked in the garden of the Prefecture on days of good weather, it often happens that she bounds like a young horse ... and we have seen her in a moment of gaiety drag five strong men.'

The winter of 1827 was particularly severe, but Zarafa flourished and quickly became a celebrity in Marseilles. It was reported: 'This animal has a very gentle disposition, and has never been seen to manifest the slightest anger or malice. She distinguishes the Arab who usually feeds her, but she does not have an unusual affection for him. She allows herself to be approached by all who come to see her.' Invitations to the prefect's dinner parties became highly prized social affairs because, afterwards, the guests would be escorted through the wind-swept gardens to her stable for a private viewing. The prefect himself was captivated by her beauty and entranced by her docility; long after she left Marseilles he continued to write with concern and affection as if she was a favourite god-daughter.

Despite her endearing attachment to people, Zarafa's relations with other animals were far from easy: horses were frightened of her and the cows, which she followed everywhere, ignored her.

By the end of February she and the cows were being exercised outside the city, events which became such a public spectacle that gendarmes were called so that her progress was not impeded. In the meantime, the authorities were considering the problem of how to get Zarafa to Paris; in comparison her journey from the

Ethiopian highlands seemed easy. It was first assumed that another sea voyage, around Gibraltar, Spain and Portugal to le Havre and up the Seine would be the answer. She had, after all, come to no harm crossing the Mediterranean. By now however, she was bigger and stronger and almost impossible to restrain if she panicked in the notoriously stormy Bay of Biscay. Another river voyage, up the Rhone was also considered. However, as spring advanced and her walks beyond the city lengthened, it was decided on 'the voyage by land'.

It is at this point that Etienne Geoffrey Saint-Hilaire enters the story. He had been one of the savants who had accompanied Napoleon on his ill-fated invasion of Egypt and had since become an eminent but elderly zoologist whose activities were greatly impaired by gout and rheumatism. This unlikely hero was appointed by the authorities in Paris to accompany Zarafa on the completion of her journey and be responsible for her safety and well-being. After many delays, Saint-Hilaire finally arrived in Marseilles on 4 May. Once there he spent some time 'studying the appearances and habits of this gigantic animal' and convincing himself that she could withstand the rigours of walking five hundred and fifty miles through France. His extensive preparations included an oilskin cloak, embroidered with the fleur de lys, to protect Zarafa from the rain and some overshoes in case her hooves began to wear down. The authorities along the projected route were instructed to provide mounted gendarmes to escort the convoy and to designate stables with headroom of at least twelve feet. Zarafa was a gift to the king so no expense was spared, no contingency overlooked.

As the rain poured down on a Sunday morning in late May, Saint-Hilaire led a strange procession; behind him were the milk cows followed closely by Zarafa with Atir holding her by a lead rope, then horse-drawn carts with all the baggage. They began the long, wet climb away from the sea and gendarmes pulled oncoming vehicles to one side to allow passage. Their drivers must have been astonished to see a giraffe wearing a raincoat.

The first stop was at Aix, a distance of some twenty miles, but Saint-Hilaire had not anticipated the toll that would be taken by the weather and terrain; by the time they arrived the entire party was exhausted – all, apart from Zarafa. They rested the following day and in gratitude to their hosts, Zarafa was exhibited to the populace. 'The crowd,' wrote Saint-Hilaire, 'was like a cavalry charge ... and the giraffe was more tired from these occupations of repose than she was from the day's march.'

Within a few days the weather had improved and the coastal uplands had flattened to a rolling patchwork of orchards, vineyards and fields; the air was filled with the herby scents of Provence and Zarafa took to browsing on the trees they passed. Progress, however, was slow and was often impeded by the never-ending crowds that lined the route; Zarafa's reputation had preceded her. Saint-Hilaire was almost overwhelmed by organisational details, by the inadequate accommodation they were offered and by the constant haggling over costs. At

Avignon he was fatigued and unwell and, with the exception of Zarafa, everyone was suffering. He therefore devised a new plan: to complete the journey down the easily navigable Saone. It had the additional advantage of being less accessible to the gawking crowds. But first he had to get approval of these changed arrangements from Paris. For reasons which have never been explained, the necessary authority was never received.

Zarafa and her entourage therefore continued along the original route through worsening weather and entered the large city of Lyons. A newspaper reported, 'Today the Giraffe toured a part of the city, accompanied by her keepers, a numerous picket of police, and a great crowd of the curious. The courteous animal did not fail to visit the Prefect, who accorded her the welcome due to a beautiful stranger'. In the same week Lyons witnessed a grisly murder, a public execution and an exhibition of 'living serpents' and other curiosities brought to the city by a couple of hucksters from London. But despite these rival entertainments, Zarafa's presence attracted a crowd of thirty thousand, by far the biggest she had experienced so far. All was going well until a horse shied at the sight of such an extraordinary animal towering over it. Zarafa bolted, dragging her handlers behind her, and Saint-Hilaire was among the many injured in the ensuing pandemonium.

With no word from Paris about his proposed new plan, Saint-Hilaire pushed on into Burgundy, with injuries now compounding his increased ill health. After three weeks on the road, tensions were breaking out among his team of different nationalities, religions and language, but the convoy struggled on. All were relieved when they finally reached Paris ten days later. In his final report Saint-Hilaire wrote that his own health was much worse than the giraffe's, in fact, ' ... it is principally the Giraffe whom the journey has marvellously benefited. She gained weight and much more strength from the exercise: her muscles were more defined, her coat smoother and glossier upon her arrival ...'. In the meantime, in far-off Greece, Ottoman forces had occupied Athens and France allied itself with Britain and Russia to expel them, thus betraying the deal with Muhammad Ali and his exotic gift.

Zarafa was installed in a greenhouse in le Jardin du Roi but the king, who desperately wanted to see his giraffe, was in the palace of Saint-Cloud. He had been kept informed of her progress since leaving Marseilles and complained bitterly that every man in France would have seen her before him, but his formidable wife, Marie-Therese d'Angouleme insisted on absolute protocol: the king must not go to Zarafa, she had to be brought to him. So after five hundred and fifty miles in forty-one days, Zarafa had to walk a total of another eighteen miles through the crush of Paris. In addition to his other maladies, Saint-Hilaire now suffered from an excruciating pain in his bladder but the king, utterly delighted with his gift and oblivious to the scientist's discomfort, kept him talking for an hour, asking for details of the journey and about Zarafa's upkeep. Atir put her through her paces to demonstrate her extraordinary gait and gallop, and the king fed her with rose petals. And so began an era of Zarafamania which influenced every sphere of fashion, became part of everyday speech and entered French folklore.

Zarafa lived for another seventeen years in her greenhouse. One set of double doors provided access to an enclosure in the open air, and another to a sheltered part of the building which was heated in winter. 'It is truly the boudoir of a little lady,' wrote Saint-Hilaire. Two ladders enabled Atir to reach a small mezzanine, where he slept within scratching distance of her head. Dressed for the part in his native robes he became quite a showman during the day, parading and grooming Zarafa for the crowds that continued to visit her. He learned French and by night he acquired quite a reputation as a ladies' man. He is long forgotten now, but in the villages and towns through which Zarafa passed, streets, squares, taverns and inns are still named la Girafe.

Author's note   The web provides much information about the king's giraffe but the main source for this story is Michael Allin's delightful book *Zarafa: The true story of a giraffe's journey from the plains of Africa to the heart of post-Napoleonic France* published in 1999 by Review

Biographies

As a former publisher, **Andrew Bax** spent much of his life issuing deadlines to busy professionals who had very little time for writing. Now he has started to write himself he wonders why none of them, as far as he knows, blew a gasket.

Janet Bolam was brought up next to the ultimate playground - a farm complete with cows, chickens, geese, a pony and resident children. Now she plays with theatre, writing and grandchildren.

Kathleen Daly lives in Oxford with a rescue border collie, a retired Riding for the Disabled horse and a physicist husband.

Ann Edwards lives in a small village in Oxfordshire. She is married with three children, has a one eyed pug, a magnificent cat, a foul tempered parrot and four hens. She likes to talk about writing and has given up cooking for watching the telly.

Wendy Greenberg (plus her husband and son) are housekeepers to 2 cats with attitude. When not tending to their every need she regularly escapes to a world of fiction - reading, writing and Ambridge. She also loves (in no particular order) the West Wing, Veuve Cliquot, good food, the sea and singing in the car.

Veronica Mackinnon is a garden designer and author. She mainly writes gardening articles for magazines but occasionally finds time to compose nonsense verse. She has two Jack Russells, two children and a husband, in order of priority.

Nichola May home educates her three children and is in her final year of a Diploma in Creative Writing. She keeps chickens and a badly behaved spaniel.

Jackie Vickers keeps neither mad hens nor crazy pets. She does, however, care about the fate of badgers and this year's fledglings. Writing about animals can provide a welcome diversion from reality.